The Lost Canoe

Isabel M Creager

To Annette with much love & good memories
Isabel (Mutti)

ISBN-10: 1493784552
ISBN-13: 9781493784554
Library of Congress Control Number: 2013921541
CreateSpace Independent Publishing Platform
North Charleston, South Carolina

DEDICATION

In this my 90th year, I dedicate this book to my family, from the American Revolution to the present day. I also want to thank the Oakmont Writers.

1

~

The sun was almost overhead in the summer sky when they first saw the canoe. It was not tied up to the homemade wharf by the mill, but had drifted further down the Susquehanna, wedging itself at a strange angle, stuck underneath a sweeper, an overhanging tree branch.

The settlers approached carefully, wary of an Indian ambush. The canoe looked so out of place. Sacks of unmilled grain lay in the bottom. A raven pecked at one of the sacks.

Coming closer, the men noticed blood across the trail, and smashed underbrush. Signs of struggle and dragging continued right up to the edge of the small creek that fed into the river. But on the other side of the creek, all traces of the canoe's owner were gone.

Upriver earlier that morning, near Forty Fort, the only sounds had been the peaceful riverflow, green oak leaves rustling, and a happily barking dog. A light mist filtered the sun on the Susquehanna, making it difficult to see clearly.

Indians had been patiently waiting along the river. They knew that, sooner or later, settlers would need to bring their grain to the grist mill. They had been watching, off an on for a few days, when they spotted two men paddling a canoe.

Eli Jackson thought, since there had been no Indian raids in recent weeks, it would be safe to leave the protection of the fort, so he had volunteered for the trip. He invited his neighbor, Jake, to go with him. Jake, a lazy, disagreeable man, would go along as a favor for Jake's wife, who was kept busy caring for their five young children and didn't need him underfoot. It was such a sweet morning when they set out, Eli found himself whistling. His wife, Ruth, had bundled a meal for them, and both men had their long guns with them.

They pulled in by the mill, and tied up, placing their guns carefully away from the water. They turned to unload the grain. That was when Eli felt the sharp tip of the Indian's knife under his right ribs. Jake was thrown to the ground, an Indian's strong hand around his neck to keep him from screaming.

Five Indians surrounded them, naked to the waist, wearing only breechcloths, belts and moccasins. Sweat oiled their coppery skins. They had taken the two white men prisoners in minutes.

Eli was terrified. His heart was beating so loudly, he was certain the Indians could hear it. He prepared to die.

One Indian, who appeared to be the leader, ordered the two settlers to remove their boots and socks. Eli quickly did as he was told. Jake was much less cooperative. He refused, struggling to keep his boots on. As a result, two of the Indians began beating Jake and roughly removed them for him, while he fought and kicked. Both men's boots were quickly thrown far out into the fast flowing river. Despite his mortal terror, Eli hated to see his one and only pair of boots wash away. He stood there in his bare feet, watching as the Indians grabbed the long guns, and the food his wife had prepared, and shoved his canoe with bags of grain far out into the strong river current. The canoe disappeared into the mist.

Eli made himself stand still and keep quiet, gazing at his captors. Jake, however, continued to loudly curse the Indians, making them so angry, they began to beat both men. Immediately, the captives were hurried off into the woods at a fast pace.

"Be quiet Jake," Eli whispered. "The more you complain, the worse we'll be treated." However, Jake didn't heed Eli's warning and, as a result, both men were struck again.

"You talk, you die," the leader told the men, as they pushed and dragged them into the creek. They were forced to walk upstream on the wet rocks for some distance, before cutting back into the woods. The Indians brushed away their tracks when they emerged from the creek. They left no footprints

Not accustomed to going barefoot, their feet were soon cut and bruised, as they were forced to run. The Indians could run for miles. They ran along deer trails, bypassing any villages and farms so as not to be seen. They were made to run throughout the rest of the long day.

~

2

~

Eli Jackson joined the Patriot army in 1776. After serving with George Washington at the Battle of Brandywine and at Valley Forge, he returned to Pennsylvania's Wyoming Valley, located along the Susquehanna River in Northeastern Pennsylvania. Eli and thirty-nine other men built a fort to protect their families from the increased Indian raids that had been a threat to both life and property. They called the place "Forty Fort."

Eli was small in stature, but strong for his five foot six height. His hair was brown and his blue eyes smiled easily, lighting his ruddy complexion. He was an outgoing, friendly man. He and his wife, Ruth, had two children, a son, Joseph, and a young daughter, Elizabeth. The family's faith had carried them through difficult times, and their love for each other was evident.

Their neighbors, Jake and Mary Rogers, were the parents of five children. Mary had been brought up on a farm, and attended a small country church. Jake, a city boy, had no use for any religion. Marriage had not been kind to Mary.

Although there had been fewer Indian attacks in recent months, the settlers continued to remain cautious. By early summer, the supply of flour was extremely low.

Ruth pushed a stray curl off her forehead, as she put flour on her hands, preparing to knead bread dough, leaving white powder on her dark hair. Her husband entered carrying firewood.

"Eli, we have very little flour left," "Yes, I know dear and I've been thinking. Things have been kinda' peaceful lately. Maybe this is a good time for me to make a trip to the mill. I could take Jake along. He certainly does nothing to help around the fort."

"I'm not sure I like that idea. I can make do for a while longer," she said, giving the dough a hard punch.

Other wives were running low as well. Someone would have to make the dangerous trip to the grist mill down river to Nanticoke. Without hesitation, Eli volunteered and asked Jake to accompany him. Ruth wasn't too pleased.

"Don't expect much help from Jake. You know how difficult it is for Mary to get him to do anything. With all those children she could no doubt get more done with him out of the way for a day. He has to be the laziest man I know."

Ruth tossed and turned all night. She got up earlier than usual and was busy preparing breakfast when Eli joined her. He was dressed ready to leave. She wiped her hands on her apron and looked at her husband. His blue eyes reflected his love for her. Ruth smiled.

"I've packed food for you. There's enough to satisfy Jake's huge appetite. I hope it will make him less troublesome and more agreeable."

"One thing he does well is eat." Eli said as the two laughed.

"You're right about that."

Eli was waiting at the river when he saw Jake dragging his feet as he approached, grumbling every step of the way.

His curly, black hair was uncombed and stuck out in every direction. His long beard was partly tucked under one corner of his shirt and his boots were dirty.

Jake stood by and watched while Eli lifted two heavy bags of grain into the canoe.

"Why in hell do we gotta' leave in the middle of the night? I ain't even had no breakfast."

When Jake boarded the canoe, he nearly tipped it over before settling his large frame in the small space.

Mary and Ruth soon arrived, carrying food. Mary appeared tired, her sweet face showed signs of stress. She walked bent forward, like a woman twice her age. A green shawl partly covered her worn dress which hung loosely on her small frame. Her long blond braids were coming undone as she turned toward Eli and gave him an appreciative nod. He understood she was grateful for a day without her husband underfoot. No words were needed.

Ruth hugged Eli after she handed him the bag of food she had lovingly prepared. Yet instinct told her Eli should not go. He felt her concern.

"Please do not worry, dear," he assured her. "We'll be home well before dark."

"Take care of yourself, Eli. Hurry home. I'll be waiting. I love you."

Jake didn't even bother to look at Mary. He stared at the setting moon as if viewing something of great importance as the canoe quietly entered the water.

The two wives stood side by side. Ruth had her arm around Mary and felt the other woman shiver. They watched until their husbands were out of sight, before returning to the fort to care for their children.

The river was high due to heavy late spring rains. The fast moving water made it easier for Eli to navigate the canoe downstream. Jake immediately fell asleep. Eli cherished the sight of the moon's spectacular reflections in the clear water of dawn. He listened to the songs of morning doves greeting a new day. He looked at his unwilling passenger and wondered what made Jake behave as he did. However, there was something about the man that drew Eli to him, and he looked forward to the time when folks could leave the fort and return to their farms. He wondered if Jake wound be happier on his farm where he could care for the animals he loved. "Jake isn't all bad," he said to himself.

Jake suddenly sat up straight. "I'm hungry. Let's eat," he shouted, as if Eli was far off.

"It's too soon," Eli replied. "We have to wait 'til after our job is done before we enjoy Ruth's lunch. Don't worry. She packed extra for you, as a reward for your help."

"Well, Eli, you know I can't work on an empty stomach."

"I'm afraid you will have to this time because it's important that we finish at the mill and return to the fort before dark."

Jake became surly and when he attempted to reach the food, he nearly tipped the canoe, almost dumping them into the river, along with the food and grain.

"Sit down, Jake. Act like a man."

Reluctantly, Jake slowly obeyed.

"The mill is around the next bend. I'm glad you rested enough this morning. It's your turn to row on the way back."

"Rowing up-stream. That's too hard, Eli. I ain't well. I can't possibly do that."

"We'll see," Eli said, as he headed toward a clearing on the bank near the mill. Colorful splashes of buttercups and bluebells were visible beside a clear, fresh stream, where it flowed into the river. Dappled early morning sunlight shone through the elm and maple trees along the shore.

Eli was happy as Jake grudgingly helped pull the canoe out of the water. It would be a long time before he would be happy again. The Indians struck.

3

~

The morning after their capture, matters only became worse. Jake was very angry and continued to fight. When he tried to run away, one young Indian immediately struck him on the back with the flat of a hatchet, then kicked him numerous times. A light rain began. But for their capture, what would have been a pleasant, sunny day suddenly turned into a frightful and rainy one.

With two Indians leading and the rest following behind, Eli and Jake were continuously forced to run. Eli obeyed, but once again, Jake rebelled. He kicked the nearest Indian in the leg and was rewarded with a swift hit on both of his legs. He lagged behind Eli, and continued to cuss as loud as possible.

"Damn you Eli. This is all your fault. I could have been home in bed where it's safe."

Angered by the outburst, and not wanting to be seen or heard, one of the Indians gestured toward Jake, as if to cut his throat.

Eli whispered, "Be quiet," and was rewarded with another angry look from Jake.

By the time they were on the main trail, Jake's face was so red he looked ready to explode. Eli was close enough to see the shape of the Indian's faces through the paint and to smell their rain-soaked, greasy deerskins. As the prisoners were hurried on, Eli listened to the steady padding of moccasins and the sound of Jake stumbling behind him. When Jake tried to speak to Eli, he was hit on the shoulder by the flat side of a tomahawk and reminded he would be killed. Their feet, unaccustomed to being bare, were soaked and bruised by unseen stones and roots.

Eli was smaller than most men, but had gained strength from having worked hard most of his forty-six years. He was also a devout Christian. Jake, on the other hand, was not in good physical condition. He was six feet tall, and overweight. When he stumbled it was difficult for him to regain his balance. The Indians grew less tolerant of Jake's behavior, and as a result, both prisoners were beaten repeatedly. They were pushed closer together and Eli was sickened by the foul body smell of the Indians ahead of him. It was getting dark and he had no idea where they were being taken. It was unfamiliar country.

The prisoners were urged to run again when passing an old beaver dam and they traveled in shallow streams for some distance so as not to leave footprints in case they were being followed. All the while, rain poured straight down on their heads. Because of the circuitous route taken, they did not make much progress the first day. Along the way both Eli and Jake were subjected to horrid threats and inhuman treatment. After many long painful hours, the Indians spoke in their own language, before the one who appeared to be the leader spoke to them in broken English.

"Stop. Make fire."

While Eli and Jake sat on the damp ground, the Indians built a fire and proceeded to squat round it, as the flames licked up in spite of the rain and thick smoke singed the lower branches of the hemlocks. Two Indians came up to

Jake, one on each side, and walked him several yards to a tree. He made no resistance though he looked big enough to handle them both. They lashed his wrists and ankles and left him lying on his back. Ignoring Eli, one remained as a sentry, and the other joined the circle around the fire. The rain had stopped. Water dripping from the trees was barely heard through the hiss of the burning wood.

Eli shivered, sitting very still on the wet grass, not wanting to attract attention to himself. He watched the Indians. He thought they looked more like queer birds than men, squatting there, with the bedraggled feathers leaning damply over their ears, and braided scalp locks, like some kind of crest, on the crowns of their heads.

After dark, Jake called to Eli, "What will they do to us?"

Before Eli had time to answer, his hands and ankles were tightly bound. The Indians carried him nearer to the fire where he lay between two blanketed Indians. The prone figures of the Indians and captives, even the two watching Indians, crouched down inside their blankets. Neither of the prisoners had any cover or protection from the rain.

They were small and quiet enough in the wilderness to bring a barred owl close. He passed over them with a silent ruffle of his feathers, turning on one wing when he reached the fire's warmth.

Eli slept from exhaustion. When he awoke during the night, the rain had stopped, there was only the drip from trees, a sound barely heard through the hiss of the burning logs. By the fire light, he could see the painting on the naked chest of the Indian beside him. The darkness came closer. Jake snored nearby and occasionally cried out in his sleep. There was nothing Eli could do.

The next day was the same. The weather changed with their continual marching. The nights grew warmer, and the lack of rain was a godsend to the captives. They no longer needed to run, and there was an element of timelessness in their march. The woods looked all alike to them. The leader appeared to be sniffing from one deer trail to another, had the air of a careful dog finding his way through strange country.

The Indians were in no hurry now, and as long as their captives kept moving at all, they left them alone. When they stopped to rest, an Indian faced Eli.

"Come here, dog," he said.

When Eli obeyed, he cocked his fire lock, put it to Eli's chest and grinned, then put his finger to the trigger. At first Eli thought these were his last moments, but he said and did nothing. Seeing that Eli paid no attention to these motions, he would open the pan, throw out the priming, and after priming anew, would put the gun to Eli's forehead, with the same furious motions as before. This went on all day. The Indian did everything he could think of to torture the small, quiet man.

Eli maintained a positive attitude, even as his body and mind were being abused. He relied on prayer to help pass the long hours. While walking, Eli continued to pray for his family. Prayer kept his mind occupied and made it possible for him to go on.

At night the Indians tied Jake to a tree, by cords around his waist. He was sitting, his back drawn tight to the tree trunk and his big body thrust forward against the cords.

In a very loud whisper, loud enough for all to hear, Jake said, "How in hell do they expect me to sleep tied up like this?" He struggled against the restraints.

Eli was too tired to reply. Fatigue settled over him like a crushing weight. He turned on his side, pulled his knees up to his chest and fell sound asleep.

The Indians slept like logs of wood laid out under their blankets. Only the one who watched sat upright, his head like a bare gourd balanced on his shoulders, and his thin face watching the coals, and listening.

4

~

Next morning early, Eli's body was stiff and lame from lying on the ground without a blanket and Jake could barely stand after he was cut loose. The Indians continued to be hard on the prisoners, dealing out frequent blows. To make matters worse, the increasing heat brought out swarms of flies and mosquitos that trailed the winding march in clouds.

Jake acquired the habit of walking bent over. His eyes ached from watching the slow progress of earth beneath his feet. When Eli looked back, the trees seemed to multiply behind him and moved together, shutting out his view of Jake. The uneven ground made small stones difficult to see. Their legs and feet showed dried blood from briars, and a trickle of fresh blood passed over Eli's ankle and ran to earth beside his instep.

That evening they reached Mehoopany where there was an encampment of Tories, who had sided with the British and hated the patriot soldiers like Eli. Eli recognized some of them as former neighbors. Happy at the first sight of familiar faces, he greeted them.

Elmer Harvey, one of the Tories, stepped forward. "I'm surprised to see you here," he said to Eli. "Glad the Indians have you,. Too bad they didn't kill you."

They were angry at Eli, who had fought in the Patriot Army and refused to join them in fighting on the side of the British. Eli was sad to think they could be so hateful.

Just before dark, Elmer's wife, Amy, came to see Eli.

"Ruth was my friend," she said. "I thought you could use these." She handed Eli an old, clean towel, and a bit of soap.

"I'm sorry Elmer is such a stubborn man. Once he sets his mind on something, he won't change. I'll keep Ruth and your children in my prayers."

"God bless you, Amy. Now I know why Ruth thought so highly of you."

The next morning as they were leaving, another Tory neighbor gave Eli some corn-bread and buttermilk. They told the Indians, "He is a brave and honest man."

The Tories paid no attention to Jake, who sat ignoring everyone. As they proceeded on the narrow path, Eli noticed that the dark coppery skin of the Indian leader was smooth and worked over his muscled shoulder blades with almost liquid freedom. The captain was a strong, healthy man.

Eli continued to observe the Indian, while Jake, having learned nothing, once again became loud and boisterous. As a result, the Indians hit both men with sticks, forcing them to run faster. Eli gritted his teeth, took a couple of deep breaths and tried to keep up.

The captives were now separated by three Indians in between, leaving no way for Eli to warn Jake to keep his mouth shut. Eli was fearful. This was worse than any battle conditions he had experienced in the army. It was all he could do to control his anger. When he fell, landing in a berry patch, tearing his clothes, he felt he might loose control, but did not. The leader, who was walking near Eli, noticed his reaction.

"You do not fear me,?" he said.

Eli was surprised to hear English, and tried to respond, but it was too difficult for him to talk due to the recurring pain in his side.

Surprised and out of breath, Eli managed to say, "You speak our language,"

"A white woman taught me when I was very young, because my father is chief."

Eli was given no time for further talk. The Indian's hawk-like eyes stared at Jake, who swore as he returned their stares. Two Indians repeatedly tormented Jake. They tripped him now and then, simply knocking him down. Jake yelled louder.

It was another long, dreadful day. Both captive's lips were cracked and dry.

When the leader stopped in the shade a short distance ahead, Eli heard the leader answer to the name, Lost Arrow, as he noticed what he thought was a mirage to the right of the path. The others seemed unaware of the clear sky, and the south wind drawing down the valley. They did not even see the stream, a deep blue sinuous cord half hidden by it's banks of high natural grass. Though he was in bad shape, Eli still had enough spirit to lift his eyes and see how beautiful it was. His clothing was muddy and torn. He was in need of a shave and his feet were swollen and painful.

The Indians got angry when Jake fell, slowing them down. Sweat poured from Jake's face as he struggled to stand. He was in bad shape after being beaten repeatedly. One eye was blackened and his face was covered with dirt and dry blood. His hair and beard, which had grown longer, were snarled and filthy.

When they reached a spring of fresh water, which flowed into a stream, Lost Arrow stopped.

"Drink," was all he said.

Grateful, Eli quickly got down on his belly and leaned into the cool, clear water. The Indians laughed at Eli's efforts as he cupped his hands and drank, soothing his parched mouth. He appreciated the opportunity, and proceeded to wash the grime from his face and hands. He was still thirsty and drank more before getting to his feet and stepping aside. Eli silently gave thanks to God for the refreshing water and the chance for the short rest.

Jake's reaction was no surprise. He stubbornly refused to drink. Instead he sat himself on the ground and glared at the Indians in defiance.

"Damn you, Damn you all to hell," he yelled, before spitting on the feet of the Indian closest to him. "Nobody can make me drink like some wild animal," he insisted.

Lost Arrow had had enough. "Take him," he ordered, pointing to Jake.

One Indian grabbed Jake by his thick hair and pulled him to his feet. A second helped drag him away, cussing and kicking. Then there was silence. Eli believed he would never see Jake again.

Chattering birds played in the trees as they passed. The breeze was sweet with the scent of green growing things, but Eli's thoughts were troubled. The day passed slowly as they traveled through picturesque Pennsylvania hills and meadows, where a profusion of colorful wild flowers grew. Under different circumstances, he would have enjoyed the trip. However, that was not the case.

Left without Jake to torment, Lost Arrow stopped Eli, cracked his fire lock, put it to Eli's chest and grinned. Once again Eli was certain he was about to die, but he said and did nothing. This action continued. All day, Eli thought he was about to die. He prayed for his family and asked God to protect each of them and to give him courage. As he lifted his eyes to unbroken blue sky, he saw a large hawk carving his solitary flight into the wind. An inner calm settled over Eli and he thought of those he loved.

It started to rain, light at first, but by late afternoon the wind picked up and the rain increased. For long, weary hours Eli did his best to kept pace with the Indians, often stumbling to keep up. Branches tore at his saturated clothes as he staggered forward. By now, his bare, raw feet were covered with mud. As darkness settled over the hills, the rain stopped.

5

~

Since their capture the prisoners had been bound every night. Now Lost Arrow gave Eli water and shared a portion of dried venison before they slept.

After that Eli felt he was given a little more consideration. Lost Arrow took Eli aside and treated his badly cut and bruised feet. He brought water and had Eli soak his feet, then he applied bear grease to the wounds and wrapped each foot in rags, tied with deer skin strips, making it easier for Eli to walk.

The summer heat added to Eli's discomfort, but it didn't seem to effect Lost Arrow.

"Where are you taking me?" Eli asked.

Lost Arrow didn't reply but noticed his prisoner put forth a lot of effort to kept up the pace, never complaining. Although Eli was much smaller than the Indian, he was proving to be as to be brave as the Tory had said.

Eli managed to remain peaceful, even as his body was being abused.

They followed the river most of the day, skirting farms to avoid being seen. Eli appreciated the natural beauty of the countryside. He heard the hum of bumblebees on wild flowers and the lazy flap of an eagle's wings as the circled the sky overhead, searching for an unsuspecting rabbit or squirrel. As they arrived near Shemongo, the long shadows of evening reflected on the water. The breeze blew warm and damp off the river, flattening the smoke of nearby Indian campfires into a gray shroud.

Indian lookouts had been watching. When they saw Lost Arrow approaching with a captive, they sent word to the village. The Indians were prepared and gathered, ready to welcome them.

As they approached the Indian Village, they were met by about thirty men. The Indians lined up on both sides of the path, each holding a stick. Lost Arrow directed Eli to run fast.

"You must run the gauntlet," he told Eli. "My brothers test you."

Eli was terrified. He froze, unable to move. Seeing Eli hesitate, Lost Arrow gave him a hard push, hurling him forward. When a young Indian tried to trip Eli, Lost Arrow was close behind and, taking him by the arm, quickly ran with him to a nearby house. His shoulder hurt where he was struck by a stick. His mood was as dark as the blackest crow that ever flew. But the Indians were impressed at the white man's courage and, although he was hit many times, Eli did not complain.

Eli was surprised when Lost Arrow touched him lightly on the arm. "We go now," he said.

The two joined a group of Indians who were eating. They gave Eli fresh cooked venison and buttermilk and left him unrestrained while they talked among themselves. Eli fell asleep.

When he awoke it was dark. He discovered Lost Arrow asleep close by. He dozed off and on the rest of the night, and dreamed of his home and family. Before he was fully awake, he pictured Ruth on the day he left. The expression on her face and the look of love in her eyes gave him courage. He recalled her fear of the trip to the mill.

The march continued. The trail grew steep and treacherous with rocks that slipped beneath his feet to roll and scatter through the brush. He felt as fragile as a dry leaf blown by the wind. When they came to a creek the Indians made him follow them for several hundred feet in cold water. At this point, the cold actually felt good against his bruised body.

Little progress was made during the cloudy morning. In early afternoon, storm clouds came up and it started to rain again and didn't let up until they arrived at another Indian encampment. They joined a group of Indians who were traveling in the opposite direction and had set up a temporary camp.

While Lost Arrow listened to the other Indians talk, he noticed how bad Eli appeared.

Eli's feet had started to bleed through the rags, and his hands had painful lacerations caused by frequent falls on the sharp rocks. He crossed his arms over his chest, hugging himself.

"I have never felt worse," he admitted to Lost Arrow, who took him where he could rest. Once again, Eli was not restricted.

"Stay here," Lost Arrow said, before leaving.

A short time later, Eli heard a commotion at the edge of the clearing. Two Indians came, half carrying, half dragging a man who had been badly beaten. Eli recognized them as the two who took Jake. Eli had thought his neighbor was dead. It wasn't until they came closer that Eli got a good look at Jake. Both of Jake's eyes were swollen shut. A fresh gash in his head was bleeding. His beard was caked with dried blood and dirt and what remained of his clothes were torn and filthy.

Eli gasped at the sight of his friend.

"Oh Jake, what have they done to you?"

Eli felt guilty because Lost Arrow had started treating him better, compared to what Jake must have suffered. If only Jake had acted differently, Eli thought.

Lost Arrow had one of the Indian women bring water and a rag and told Eli, "Wash your friend."

They offered Jake food, but he was in and out of consciousness, and unable to eat. Other Indians, both men and women sang, beat drums and danced around the two of them all night. The short times Jake was awake, he and Eli couldn't communicate because of the noise. Before daylight, Jake was taken away again.

Lost Arrow decided to join a number of Indians traveling in the same direction. No sooner were they on their way when a party of renegade Indians appeared from behind some large rocks where they had been hiding. One was exceedingly fierce and warlike. There were black lines painted on his forehead and cheeks, below a headband from which an eagle feather protruded. His long hair hung loose past his shoulders. A bright piece of red cloth was tied around his upper arm.

With great fury, the Indian grabbed Eli and began to strip off all of his clothes, giving them to one of his comrades. Eli was puzzled when Lost Arrow showed no signs of anger and did nothing to interfere. He walked naked for about a hundred yards, when a second Indian came up to him yelling, "Yankee! Yankee!" and raised his knife as though he was going to cut Eli in half, but struck him on the back with his fist instead.

Eli was not a large man, and now, naked, he thought he must look as skinny as a starving coyote, and he felt nearly as skittish. He was terribly embarrassed to be without clothes.

"It is is inhuman to make me go on like this," Eli said, hoping they understood.

The other Indians departed as quickly as they had arrived. Only then did Lost Arrow reluctantly give Eli a faded red shirt from a sack he carried. It reached below his knees and was so large he had to fold the sleeves back. The smallest breeze reminded him of his nakedness underneath. However, it was better than being naked.

The warm sun shone bright from an azure sky, in which billowy clouds floated, but Eli remained chilled deep inside. As always, he turned to his faith for support and hope.

The rest of the morning was more peaceful, as they traveled through bottom land. Spruce and pine trees were plentiful, and the familiar scent calmed Eli. Many animals roamed the forest.

In an attempt to engage Lost Arrow in conversation, Eli said, "Tell me, how do you trap and hunt?"

After pausing and deciding Eli was really interested, Lost Arrow responded. "We believe in Mother Earth. We have all we need, animals are plentiful, but we take only what we need. My people ask the animal's forgiveness when we take it's life. Every part of the animal is used. White men kill for pleasure and fur." He picked up the pace and said no more.

6

~

Under different circumstances, it would have been a fine day for a walk. The natural beauty of the Pennsylvania countryside was a treat to the senses. Along with the fragrant smell of pine, came happy memories of home. Eli's thoughts puzzled him. He was filled with mixed emotions. He was lonely, sad, dirty and hungry, yet he was grateful to be alive.

By noon they reached a place hidden enough to build a fire. When Lost Arrow began to gather firewood, Eli started to do the same, while two of the Indians went off in search of game. Lost Arrow was surprised and pleased by the help. Eli began to feel that Lost Arrow was really a caring person. He treated his followers well and had recently shown kindness to Eli.

Lost Arrow told Eli, "you rest," while he built a fire in a circle of stones others had used before. Too tired to even think of escaping, Eli took advantage of the peace and quiet, and slept until the cooking aroma wakened him.

Eli said a silent grace for the food he was about to eat. He knew his body needed to be nourished if he were to survive. Their meal consisted of pheasant, a rabbit and some blackberries, but Eli ate only small portions because his stomach refused more.

While they were eating, Eli noticed a stranger. He didn't talk to anyone, just stood leaning against a tree at the edge of the clearing. He stared at Eli, never changing his grim expression, which made the long, ugly scar on his left cheek stand out. Eli felt intimidated and was anxious to move on. The Indians, however, ignored the man as they continued enjoying their feast, licking the grease from their fingers.

Fed and rested, the Indians walked at a slower pace. Lost Arrow didn't seem to mind that Eli lagged a short distance behind the others. Thinking about his family, Eli was surprised when suddenly a hard blow to the back of his head knocked him off balance. Turning quickly, he recognized the scarred face of the young, hateful Indian who had followed them.

Before he could move, he was hit on the other side of his head and sent sprawling in the dirt. Dazed, Eli shook his head trying to clear his vision and stop the ringing in his ears. He moved quickly to avoid being kicked as he struggled to get back on his feet. This happened so fast that, by the time Lost Arrow turned around, the Indian had grown tired and was walking away. The remainder of the day some of the Indians walked behind Eli.

Late in the afternoon, Eli noticed the Indians were watching the angles of the sun. The trail they had taken turned into a second trail and the second joined into a third, each seemed wider and more traveled than the last. The third trail entered a well-beaten path that dipped downward sharply to a lake and followed along the shoreline under tall trees. He could see the clear, blue water between the trees.

The Indians talked to each other, pointing to the sun and trees along the bank. He thought he heard the same word repeated, "Oneidas." Whenever the Indians uttered it, their voices seemed to rise.

Lost Arrow covered Eli with a ragged blanket that night, where he lay and gazed up at the heavens. Here he was, away from his family, who needed and depended on him. He had already lost track of how many times the sun had risen and set since his capture. He viewed the stars through the trees and thought about Ruth and his children.

He hoped Joseph, his sixteen year old son, was looking after them. Who would take care of his family, he wondered? What about his livestock? Would Ruth remain at the fort or return to her parent's home in Connecticut? Too many questions for his tired mind. He fell into a fretful sleep on the hard ground.

The next morning, the Indians busied themselves painting their faces, which they examined in a piece of broken mirror. They took turns braiding each others scalp locks. Excitement surrounded the Indians as they prepared to enter the town.

"This is Queen Catherine's town," Lost Arrow informed Eli.

Eli had learned of Catherine Montour from his father, who had admired the woman's strength and courage. Eli knew she was half Indian, educated, spoke English, and was known to be a peace maker, convincing the Indians many times not to fight the white man.

By the time they reached the town, Eli was so weak and tired from the long day's walk, he could hardly stand. Lost Arrow took him directly to Catherine's house. Eli had heard many stories about the famous squaw. He wished he were more presentable.

Several Tory men sat outside the door of Catherine's house.

"Where did you find this man?" one asked.

"At the white man's grist mill," Lost Arrow replied, feeling very proud of himself.

Upon hearing the conversation, Catherine appeared, to see who was there. She looked first at Eli and, after seeing his terrible condition, she directed her attention to Lost Arrow.

Addressing him in perfect English, she said. "Lost Arrow, you are a disgrace. What would your honorable father think of the way you have treated this man?"

Her dark eyes blazed with disgust. She was disappointed. She was ashamed of Lost Arrow for the first time.

Lost Arrow, at a loss for words, and eyes downcast, quietly answered.

"He is my prisoner. I had to make him run. He is a brave man and will serve well," he added.

Eli stood there. He felt both uncomfortable and embarrassed, as he listened to the exchange of words between the two, and wondered what his fate would be.

Catherine turned to a woman standing near her, "Shadow Lake, take Eli where he can have some privacy to bathe and dress. Try to find some suitable clothes for him."

The younger woman seemed happy to oblige and set out to do as she was asked. Eli thanked Catherine before following Shadow Lake. He was touched by Catherine's sensitivity.

Lost Arrow remained standing beside Catherine.

"I expected better of you. Go, and make sure that this man is properly cared for. As soon as he is ready, take him to a place in my house to sleep. Do you understand?"

Humbled and ashamed, Lost Arrow faced Catherine. "I'm truly sorry," he said.

Much later, Shadow Lake returned with Eli. He was dressed in some of her oldest son's clothes. The moccasins she brought had belonged to her husband. He looked very tired and worn out as he faced Catherine.

"It's the best I could do," Shadow told Catherine.

Catherine looked Eli over. The clothes were a little snug, but he was clean and covered. "Thank you. You have done well."

Eli appreciated being properly clothed, and her welcoming smile made Eli feel better. It reminded him of his mother's smile, when he was a small boy.

"I'm glad you are here, and sorry for the way you were treated. You will sleep on my house tonight. What are you called?"

"My name is Eli," he replied. "What am I to call you?" he asked with respect.

"Everyone calls me Catherine."

"Thank you for your kindness, Catherine."

Eli was concerned about Lost Arrow and hoped he wouldn't be punished too harshly.

"Please, do not be hard on Lost Arrow. He is still young, but he is a good man. He treated me better the last few days."

"There is no excuse for his behavior. He was brought up to know better. However, I will consider what you've said."

"It is good to hear English spoken," he told her.

"I also speak French," Catherine explained. "My father, Frontenac, was French Canadian and was governor of Quebec at one time."

After sitting quietly for a few minutes, she continued. "My mother was a Huron Indian. She was the one who saw that I was well cared for and given an education." Eli admired Catherine and thought she was a very gracious and intelligent woman.

7

~

That night, Eli slept on one of the large bearskin rugs in Catherine's home. He heard crickets chirping, and an owl's hoot echoing through the trees and felt safe for the first time since his capture.

The next morning, Lost Arrow appeared, and sat on the floor beside Eli as he slept. Lost Arrow had trouble waking Eli, who couldn't remember where he was or what he was doing there.

"I'm sorry to wake you," Lost Arrow said. "I came to apologize, I should not have been so hard on you, Eli. Your friend, Jake, made me angry but it was wrong of me to make you suffer for his actions."

Eli was groggy. He sat up partway, "I'll be alright," Eli managed to reply.

"Catherine has been kind to me. She promised to tell me where I'm to be sent from here. Will you take me to her?"

It was the first night Eli had slept in shelter. With the exception of his painful feet, and the ache in his back where the tomahawk struck him, he felt more rested. As he washed his face in cold water, he thanked God for a new day. He felt blessed.

Indians and Tories appeared to live together in the town, peacefully. Children and dogs played in a common area, near Catherine's house.

Catherine was pleased to see Eli. She had been waiting to talk to him and greeted him warmly.

"Good morning, Eli."

"Good morning Catherine," Eli replied.

Catherine was a large woman. She was the color of honey. Her eyes were a somber black and her face, with it's high cheekbones, was grooved with deep wrinkles, she stood straight and tall, giving her a regal appearance. Her long black braids, streaked with gray, covered some elegant beadwork on her tunic. She wore a knee length skirt of soft deerskin. Her moccasins and leggings were embroidered with beads of every color. Along with several bead necklaces, she wore an amulet, a charm believed to ward off evil spirits.

Catherine seemed to enjoy talking to Eli, who listened intently, hoping to learn as much as possible about her and her life with the Indians. She proceeded to tell him how, when she was ten years old, she too had been taken by Seneca Indians.

"After I lived here and worked for two years, I was forced to marry an Indian. I did not love this man. We had two sons and a daughter, but I refused to acknowledge his name."

Catherine stopped talking when Lost Arrow arrived. He no longer wore a loincloth but instead he had on deerskin leggings with fringe along the outside, along the vertical seam, and on his moccasins. He wore a deer-skin band on his right arm, half way between his elbow and shoulder. His headband held a large eagle feather.

"I was about to explain to Eli that two of my trusted friends will be escorting him to Appletown tomorrow."

Catherine directed her attention to Eli. "Do you ride?" She asked.

"Yes, I do. I was raised on a farm and have been around horses all my life."

"That is good, as I have arranged for three horses. However, you look as if you could benefit from a second restful night before leaving. You are to be adopted by my dear friend, Sukee. I've known her for many years. You will replace her grandson, who was killed by white men."

Eli had no idea what was expected of him so he made no reply.

"There is always food available. Eat small amounts frequently to help get your strength back," Catherine added.

Eli was not restrained in any way. He sat outside Catherine's house, watched, listened and began to feel stronger. A few old Indian women seemed to be caring for a group of very young children, who played around the village center. The children wore almost no clothing. Their little brown bodies looked well nourished. With their straight, black hair they all looked alike to Eli.

Tory men sat on a log bench where they talked and smoked. Eli walked to a large elm tree and sat with his back resting against it's solid trunk. He heard enough of their conversation to learn there had been some recent unsuccessful attempts by captives to escape. However, he didn't like hearing what happened to them.

For many days on the trail, Eli had had thoughts of escape. Now, with the Indian's plan for him set in place, he must watch for opportunities. He prayed for a long time while resting, and thanked God for Catherine's kindness. He asked for courage to face each day and, as always, he placed his loved ones in God's hands.

It was a clear, bright morning when two Indians, with Eli riding between them, headed north on their way to Appletown. Eli hoped he would arrive safely at his destination, as Catherine had promised. Otherwise, he might have been more fearful of the two large, muscular Seneca warriors.

During the ride, no words were exchanged. Eli wondered if they spoke little English or were simply not talking. From recent experience and from stories he had heard about how the Seneca Indians were the most feared of all the Iroquois, he treated them with respect.

As the hours passed, Eli became uncomfortable, having been accustomed to using a saddle, and had to concentrate on not slipping off the blanket that covered the back of the gentle horse.

The Indians rode bareback. Once again he was thankful for the trousers Shadow Lake had given him. Eli thought riding might have been easier than walking, but was determined not to complain. It was a big improvement over walking. He thought of his own horses and hoped his son was taking care of them.

It was easy to ride three abreast across expansive meadows but, when they reached the hills where trees thickened, they entered a steep, narrow trail. After traveling many miles, they stopped by a waterfall long enough to rest the horses, and eat dried venison, corn cakes, and the apples Catherine had provided. Eli was given equal amounts of food, which he ate in silence. He thought about meals at home with his family, talking to each other and enjoying the time together, and wondered, as he often did, how they were managing.

It was nearly sunset when they reached Appletown. Eli's legs were so numb from straddling the horse all day. He embarrassed himself when he slid off his horse, landing hard on his bottom.

A handsome Indian laughed as he came to greet Eli.

"I am Tracking Wolf. Lost Arrow is my cousin."

Eli looked up at the tall Indian standing over him.

"You are to stay with me," he told Eli, giving him his hand. "Come," he said and directed Eli to a wooden structure, called a longhouse. It was a sturdy building, framed with saplings and covered with elm bark. Eli estimated it to be about twenty-five wide and two hundred feet long.

As they entered, Eli adjusted to the semidarkness of the interior, until he could see that there was a door at each end, but no windows. There were separate cubicles on either side.

"I live here with other members of my tribe. We share space in separate sections and use the same cooking fire outside in summer. In the winter a fire is kept going in the center of the building for both heat and cooking." Tracking Wolf explained.

They went along a center hallway with a number of raised platforms sectioned off on both sides. There were reed mats on the floor, and pelts to soften seats and beds. Clothes were hung on walls, or stored neatly in bins and baskets. When the reached a space about halfway, Tracking Wolf stopped.

"You may stay here," he told Eli. "This is my space."

Very grateful, Eli thanked Tracking Wolf.

Since a message from Catherine had been sent, saying that Eli was a good man and could be trusted, he was given food and a blanket, and made welcome.

Outside Indians began to sing.

"What are they singing?" Eli ask.

"Each person sings his own words. It is our way of self expression, a way of saying how and what we feel. Our songs have the melodies of nature" Eli thought it was an interesting concept.

"You are free to move about and rest. Sleep here whenever you wish. You will not be disturbed."

Eli thanked God for the food and the safe haven. He remained seated on the soft pelt in Tracking Wolf's area. He couldn't resist his tiredness, and decided to take a nap on the soft pelt.

8

~

Other members of the tribe came and went throughout the day. Children laughed and played, making noise, but Eli slept. It wasn't until late afternoon, when Tracking Wolf returned from fishing, that he found Eli where he had left him.

Shaking Eli gently, Tracking Wolf said, "Eli, time to get up and move around. You must have been more tired than I thought. You have slept all afternoon."

Eli could not believe his nap had taken so long. How could he still feel sleepy, he wondered? He remained in the village with the Indians for three more days. The first morning he walked along a small lake adjacent to the village. No one bothered him as he wondered around, searching for a place to be alone with his thoughts and prayers.

When Eli discovered a high cliff of rocks, with a sheltered area underneath, he crawled inside. From here, he could see anyone approaching. It provided just enough room for him to lie down. After the long gruesome days since his capture, he longed for a quiet place where he could rest. He slept off and on, and sometimes dreamed of Ruth. Once he awoke sweating and in a state of exhaustion, having dreamed he was trying to save his family from being killed by Indians.

On the second day, when Eli started toward the lake, he noticed unusual activities. Tracking Wolf explained that they were preparing for one of their seasonal celebration or "doings." "This one is the Green Corn Dance." Eli stayed to watch the Indians dance and beat drums until the steady rhythm caused him to nod off. He retreated.

While living there, Eli attended a Seneca worship service. He wished to learn more about the Indians and followed others to the central building where the service for the Longhouse Religion was held. Handsome Lake was the religious prophet associated with this practice, which was conducted in the Seneca language.

Eli understood only a few words, and thought the speaker talked too long. He sat on one side of the room with the men, while the women sat on the other side. Immediately after hearing the speech, the Indians hung a dog on a high pole and burned another at the foot of it. Eli loved animals and this made him feel sick to his stomach. He got up and walked out.

Tracking Wolf followed him. "Why did you leave?" he asked Eli.

"Killing those poor dogs bothers me," Eli said. "Why do they do that?"

Tracking Wolf tried to explain, "Indians believe it brings good luck against the Yankees."

Eli thought, "I cannot see how such cruelty could ever make a difference," then decided he'd better be quiet.

The third and last morning, Tatsuwha, an elderly Indian, came looking for Eli. His skin was deeply etched with tiny lines. He wore only a loincloth and walked with a limp and had a jagged scar on his right thigh. Tatsuwha spoke English.

"Call me Joe." he said. "Catherine sent me to take you to your grandmother in Appletown."

Puzzled, Eli asked Joe, "How can I have a grandmother here?"

"You are to replace Sukee's grandson, who was killed by soldiers. She is an old woman, a leader in her tribe. She will see that you are treated well."

Eli left with the Indian later that day. He was glad to be able to converse in English, and talking helped pass the time, as they headed to what would be Eli's new home.

Joe told Eli about Sukee's family. "Sukee is raising three girls," he said. "the oldest, her granddaughter is eighteen. The two younger ones are cousins, about ten and twelve."

"Maybe I should learn some Seneca words if I am to live with her," Eli said.

"Yes, that would be helpful, but most of her family speaks English."

Before they arrived in Appletown, a younger version of Joe came to meet them. "What are you doing here my son?" Joe asked the boy.

"Sukee wanted to make sure her new grandson was coming today. She has been anxiously waiting."

Eli was impressed, but also concerned. He wondered why he was so special and hoped he would not disappoint her.

The three entered Appletown soon after, and Eli was taken directly to Sukee. Joe introduced Eli. "This is Sukee, your grandmother." Then turning to the tallest of the three girls, he said, "This is your sister, Cornflower and these two younger ones are your cousins, Willow and Fawn."

The three girls stood silently observing their new relative closely.

Cornflower was charming. She shyly regarded Eli with large, dark expressive eyes that missed nothing. Her olive complexion complemented her long, shiny black hair that cascaded past her waist. Her knee length dress of softest doeskin, was decorated with tiny colored beads. Her legs and feet were bare.

Sukee had been waiting patiently, a welcome smile lighted her weathered old face. She appeared to be truly happy to meet Eli. She came forward and greeted Eli with a hug, which surprised him a great deal. He was almost the same height which made it easier. A tiny smile escaped Eli's tired face. Sukee held his arm while other Indians stood by, their eyes fixed on their new relative. Soon Joe took Eli to meet more relatives.

As they walked away Joe said, "You will soon become an Indian yourself. You will now live as one of us."

Somehow, his vision of Cornflower remained. He tried to listen to his guide, but thoughts of Ruth and his love for her also filled his mind while Joe continued to talk.

"You can go wherever you like, but, if you try to escape you will be killed."

Eli cast aside any immediate plans to leave.

9

~

That first night in Sukee's house, Eli felt less frightened, but remained uncertain about his continued safety. He worried about how long-range plans, made by the Indians, would effect his family. It was late when he managed to sleep.

The next morning Eli was awakened to the sound of children's voices. Outside he was told to help himself to the food kettle, located in the center of an open area where a fire was kept burning. He served himself hot cornmeal mush using one of several gourds set out for that purpose. While he ate, he watched children running and playing together, making him miss his children even more.

These Seneca Indians were farmers. The young men hunted and fished, while a few elderly men helped the women do the gardening and care for the small children. The older children served as lookouts, keeping the birds and other pests away from the fields.

All the Indians contributed to the production of food. The gardens were planted in straight rows, similar to the way Eli had always done. He made himself useful by pulling weeds. The women seemed surprised at how quickly and willingly the little white man worked. He silently labored alongside them until it was time for their one big meal of the day. The rest of the day there was a large pot of soup, and wheels of corn bread, available whenever they were hungry. Eli was still unable to eat very much at a time, so this worked very well for him.

A very elderly woman appeared to do most of the cooking. Eli had been observing her and, since she always seemed to work alone, decided to ask her to teach him how she prepared different food. Her name was Sun Spirit. She had a bad curve in her spine, which caused her to walk bent forward. Wisps of thin, white hair stood out above her sun ravaged face and her old arthritic hands worked miracles with food, day after day.

Not knowing what to expect and, having noticed that Indian men did not cook, he approached Sun Spirit. "Will you show me how to cook your way?" he asked in his newly attempted Seneca language.

A quick smile brightened her face at Eli's unusual request. The inner beauty that shone through her eyes gave her a quality Eli could not define. He understood why she was called Sun Spirit. She motioned for him to join her beside a large cook pot where she had been seasoning a venison roast.

As Sun Spirit continued stirring she explained to Eli, "I will soon add these smooth stones to the pot. They will heat while the food cooks and help keep it hot longer, especially in the time of the big snows. "We have boiled our food for many generations."

Slowly, over the following days, Sun Spirit let Eli help.

"My people use corn in many ways, along with beans and squash from our garden, As you already know, we use gourds for bowls."

The kindly Indian picked up a medium sized gourd and served Eli.

"Sometimes the meat is roasted over hot coals and other times it is cooked on a spit."

The other women of the tribe found Eli's behavior unusual, but accepted it because it appeared to please Sun Spirit.

The men continued to provided fresh meat and fish. The women skinned the animals and prepared the hides to be used in a variety of ways. Some meat was eaten raw, but Eli preferred his meat well-done. Other parts of the animal were boiled, smoked, or dried to be used later.

Sun Spirit enjoyed Eli's company.

"In summer we pick berries, blackberries mostly and what few raspberries and loganberries we find," she told Eli. "After frost comes, we collect maple sugar and, always, there is much work to do."

Eli learned quickly as he worked with Sun Spirit, and was becoming a part of the Indian's daily life. When a deer was killed, the man who took it's life would kneel where the animal fell and gave thanks to the animal's spirit and the Creator for providing it. The Indians always apologized to the animal for taking it's life and would leave something in its place for the animal's family; corn or a small piece of salt lick. Every part of the animal was used, wasting as little as possible, out of respect.

Some of their practices Eli found to be inconceivable. After a deer was killed, the Indians ate the entrails and drank the fresh, warm blood. Eli politely declined when offered this delicacy. They never emptied the contents of the intestines, but boiled all together and ate everything.

After Eli was captured, he was often hungry. But when observing some of the Indian's methods, especially meat, he ate only fish and vegetables. Finally, as everyone's hunger became overwhelming, he noticed how much meat they ate when it was available. Sun Spirit encouraged Eli to taste the meat and, when he did, he had to admit the meat was good. Realizing he wanted to survive, he started to eat whatever was offered.

Both Sun Spirit and Sukee were pleased to see Eli eating more. In the evenings, Sukee liked to talk to Eli about what he had done during the day. As her grandson, Eli hoped his accomplishments made her happy.

“You have done well Eli,” she told him. “My family is proud of you.”

Eli didn’t know exactly how to answer. He still harbored a strong desire to escape.

“I am grateful for how good you have treated me.”

They were interrupted at the sound of Sun Spirit singing with glee. The hunters had just returned from a hunting trip with a large wild hog. The only time one was available was when it died of cold or hunger.

Eli watched as the Indians first burned off the hair, then cooked its intestines and all, simply squeezing out the contents before throwing it into the kettle. Eli was reluctant at first, but after Sun Spirit gave him a sample he agreed with Sukee that it was tender and sweet.

“It tastes better when I don’t see it being prepared.,” he smiled at Sukee and Sun Spirit.

“How do you expect to learn if you don’t watch?” Sun Spirit roared, her tiny body shaking with laugher.

“No look– No cook.” She said to Eli. “You are funny”

Eli frequently thought of the hardy meals his mother had prepared when he was growing up on the farm, and how Ruth had worked hard to fix nourishing meals for him and their children. He worried and wondered who was supplying Ruth with food in his absence.

On Eli’s farm he had a large vegetable garden and numerous fruit trees, a flock of chickens and two milk cows. He wondered if he would ever see his farm again.

Sukee, noticed Eli’s sad expression. She placed her hand on his arm.

"Do not be unhappy, she said, trying to guess at his sadness. "We will not make you eat anything you don't like."

Sukee and Sun Spirit were elders of the tribe and had lived to experience many changes. Both women were hard working. Friends since childhood, they managed to guide their people, and keep tribal problems to a minimum.

Sun Spirit was happy and out-going. In spite of constant arthritic pain in her spine, she never complained and had a smile and kind word for everyone. It was difficult for her to get out of bed in the morning, but once she started cooking, bent low over her cooking pots, she was in her element. She wore her thinning white hair in a single braid secured with a red ribbon. Though her face was lined with wrinkles from sun and age, the twinkle in her dark eyes revealed a youthful soul.

Eli liked hearing her hum while she prepared food. Sometimes, she sang in a strange tongue. Her mind seemed to be far away. Eli enjoyed listening to the lilting melody but always remained quiet, hoping she would continue.

Sukee was a strong, thoughtful leader, highly respected by the tribe, as well as by her family. Eli felt her strength, the kind of strength his own mother possessed. When she smiled her dark eyes sparkled. Usually her gray hair hung in long braids, partly covering the colorful beads on her tunic. Sukee's stature was one of distinction. She walked erect, her head high, steadfast in her determination to serve her people.

10

~

One morning Sukee thought Eli seemed unhappy.

"Eli, I know how hard you have been working and I think it's time for you to rest and renew your spirit. Go where you can find peace and quiet."

"Thank you. I would like that. I will be at the cave by the lake. If you need me, I'll be there," Eli replied.

"Yes, I know the place, a perfect location. May your spirit find the peace you seek."

"Wait," Sun Spirit called as she slowly approached.

She surprised Eli by giving him a deerskin pouch containing dried meat, corn bread and fruit. "Here is enough food for a few days."

After hesitating a moment she looked at Eli. "I will miss you," she said, blushing like a school girl, as Eli watched her turn and slowly walk away. He felt the love in her voice.

"Thank you, Sun Spirit," Eli called to her parting back.

Growing up, whenever Eli was worried, afraid or unhappy, he would go somewhere where it was quiet, to be alone in nature with God. Only then did he feel that all was as it should be, in the refreshing beauty of nature.

When he reached the cave, Eli gathered several bunches of tall, fragrant grass to make a bed. After placing the food pouch farther back in the cave where it was cooler, he relaxed. He sat quietly while looking at the calm view of the lake below and meditated. He thanked God for the opportunity to be alone. He prayed for his family, asking God to keep them safe and realized Sukee was right. He was tired.

After Eli took a long nap, he went for a walk. As he passed the garden where the women were busy hoeing weeds, one turned and looked at him. He recognized Cornflower. When Eli looked back and smiled, she quickly lowered her eyes and continued hoeing weeds.

The scent of grasses in the meadows, and the pungent pine and spruce trees in the dark, cool forest were refreshing. The bird songs, and the serene beauty of the trees and water helped ease the weariness he had been feeling.

All these things also reminded him of his own home and family. Eli couldn't help thinking about the possibility of escape. On his walks, he paid close attention to the paths he took and wondered which one might lead him safely away. Then he remembered the threat of death if he were to be caught and decided to remain--at least until he found the perfect escape route.

Some time later, when Eli was thinking of Ruth and the life they'd had, he wondered whether or not they would ever be together in the future. Something new was troubling him. He realized he had grown close to Sukee and the others. He cared for them. They had become dear to him. If he never managed to escape, would he be happy spending the rest of his life with the Indians? If he left, would he wonder if their lives were safe? He didn't know.

Eli returned after a week, looking and feeling refreshed.

Sukee greeted him. "Welcome home," she said when he arrived.

"It's good to be home," he said without realizing it was a natural response.

"Sun Sprit was not her usual self while you were away. I do not remember her ever reacting that way before, but then you were the first person to offer help with the cooking."

"I like Sun Spirit. She makes everyone feel better. Not only for her ability to prepare good tasting food, but by her endearing personality."

"Now that you are back I want you to start spending time with other Indian families. Cornflower, Willow and Fawn will miss you in the evenings, but you need to get acquainted with other members of our tribe."

Eli didn't know how to reply, so he said nothing. The women looked up to Eli. The cousins giggled when he teased them, calling them Buttercup and Daisy. They coaxed him to tell stories about his former life and family.

Eli was constantly reminded of those he had been forced to leave behind. Wise old Sukee was aware of this. She knew it was time for her adopted grandson the spend time with others, especially men his age. She went to find Eli.

An old Indian from another Iroquois tribe spent several days in Appletown. He found Eli to be a interested listener and proceeded to recount many of his life's experiences. Sukee found the two sitting on the ground. She was impressed at how comfortable Eli appeared as he took in every word the old man said about Indian life.

"When we Indians kill meat, we eat it all. When we dig roots we make only little holes. When we burn grass for grasshoppers, we do not ruin things. We shake down acorns and pine nuts, we do not chop down the trees. We only use the dead wood. But the white people plow up the ground, pull down trees, kill everything. The white people pay no attention. How can the spirit of the earth like white man? Everywhere the white has touched it is sore."

Eli stood when he saw Sukee.

"Do you need me?" he quickly asked.

"Lost Arrow has returned from a successful hunt and is ready to celebrate with a game of Lacrosse," Sukee told him. "He would like you to join him."

"I don't know how. I had to work and had little time for games."

"Then it's time you start. Come with me," she said happily.

Eli reached down and shook the hand of the man who had told him many interesting things about Indian life.

The old man smiled. "We talk more soon," he told his new friend.

On the way to the playing field, Lost Arrow quickly explained the rules of the game. "It's not difficult," he assured Eli. "Lacrosse had been played here for centuries, long before the white men came to our land."

After a slow beginning, Eli did well. A fast runner, he helped his team win the game, which pleased his new friends.

"I told you it was fun," Lost Arrow said, placing his arm around Eli's shoulder, making him feel welcome.

Eli had to agree. "I had a good time," he told Lost Arrow.

Each day Eli became more integrated into Indian life and culture. He not only participated in sports, but found their dances enjoyable as well. The dances and music were quite different from those familiar to him. Indians never danced in pairs, but in groups, stomping their feet as they danced in circles. Eli attempted to follow the men's dance steps which were much more expressive than those of the women. The women clapped and sang, repeating the same words over and over, like a chant, as they danced at a slower pace.

As the dance continued long into the night, Eli noticed Cornflower. She danced with such grace he couldn't stop watching. It were as if the tempo of the music was timed to her every move.

As Sukee's granddaughter, Cornflower worked with the other women. Eli had paid little attention to her, until now. As she danced he became aware of her natural beauty, the way she moved with the grace of a swan, gilding across a lake. Her long hair hung loose and seemed to glow as she swirled in the moonlight. Her brown legs and feet were bare. Dressed as she was, in her native clothing, she resembled a painting he had once admired of an Indian princess.

Eli thought of Ruth and the familiar fiddle music played by friends and neighbors, so different from that of the Indians. He longed for her. He remembered how Ruth liked to sing as she worked. Her lovely voice was indeed music to his ears, as she sang hymns and songs. Eli didn't sing, but when he was working alone in the fields, he found himself humming some of those tunes.

11

~

In late Fall, Eli suddenly became very ill with a high fever and was moved to a place where Sukee could see to his care. "Your sister and cousins will help look after you," she promised Eli.

For the next ten days Eli was delirious. He neither knew nor cared what was happening to him. He was fed berry juice and a special broth made by Sun Spirit. Although the creek was but a few feet away, Cornflower walked half a mile every day to get spring water, which she carried in a deerskin bag. The water was known to have medicinal and healing qualities.

Sukee's family had become very fond of Eli and when he was heard crying out in the night, they did their best to comfort him. He would awake thinking he was with Ruth.

"Ruth, come here. Where are you? I need you. I love you."

Sukee decided Eli should not be left alone during the lengthening, dark nights. She summoned Cornflower, who had often helped care for other sick members of the tribe. "I want you to stay with Eli. The next time he has disturbing dreams, try to comfort him."

Cornflower had always been an obedient child. However, she was also very shy. Since Eli's arrival she had remained in the background watching, but seldom speaking to him, unlike the cousins, who followed him around, asking Eli to tell them stories. Cornflower did as Sukee asked, and that night she sat near where her patient lay, doing her best to stay awake. Toward morning, when Eli became restless, she changed the cool compresses on his forehead and softly sang an old Seneca lullaby until he settled down.

The third night, when Eli was extremely restless, Cornflower lay down next to him and patted his arm while talking softly. Once, as he turned, one of Eli's arms came to rest on Cornflower's warm body. Assuming it was Ruth, he tightened his arm around her and pulled her close. Cornflower stiffened. When, just before dawn, Eli's fever broke, he was surprised to find Cornflower asleep beside him.

She didn't return the following night and, as he recovered, he often wondered why she was there in the first plaće, but never asked.

Cornflower was embarrassed. The emotions she experienced, lying so close to Eli made her shiver, as she remembered him holding her close. She tried to avoid being wherever Eli might be present. Nothing had happened between them, but she was concerned about what he must think of her.

When French Catherine got word that Eli had been very sick, she made the journey to see him. When she arrived, she found him resting under a large maple tree near the center of the village. a blanket covering his legs, As she greeted Eli, she thought he looked pale.

"Here you are," she said. Pleased to see him out in the fresh air. "When Sukee sent Tracking Wolf with the message that you weren't well, I felt the need to visit."

Eli was so surprised to see Catherine, he didn't know what to say.

"You are very thoughtful, Catherine, but Sukee and the others have taken good care of me. They have all been very kind, I don't know how I can ever thank them. They are my family."

Looking at this humble man, Catherine asked, "Is there anything you need, anything I can do for you?"

Eli hesitated. "I would appreciate some writing materials, if possible," he replied.

"That will not be a problem, as I'm going on to Niagara. I can find things there and can deliver them to you on my way back."

Eli brightened visibly. His simple needs, and his appreciation of help were evident. He looked forward to keeping a journal of his activities here in Appletown. "You must write to me Eli. Someone will deliver your letter."

When Eli stood to bid her good bye, Catherine saw the look of gratitude on his face and knew he would be a survivor in spite of adversity. "Be kind to him," Catherine said to Sukee as they walked to where Catherine's horse waited patiently for it's rider. Catherine and her two Indian guides, their mission completed, were given food for their trip before departing.

Eli watched until the trio was out of sight, then sat for some time in contemplation. The Indians had been sincere in their efforts to include him in their lives, as if he had been born one of them. He couldn't help but wonder if white men, who referred to the Indians as "savages", would adopt an Indian in the same way he had been adopted. He felt certain they would not. The thought disturbed him.

It was several weeks before Catherine returned. She not only brought paper and pens for Eli, she also brought a plant, sweet flag. She explained how he was to steep it in water and drink it to help make him stronger. Catherine told Sukee that Eli was to be given more freedom to do as he wished.

When Eli first arrived in Appletown he had nothing to read and spent most of his time in the woods. As his health permitted, he endeavored to spend the first of each month alone in fasting, prayer and meditation. His Indian family thought this behavior was strange, but Sukee told them Eli was free to follow his beliefs.

As weeks passed, many Tories passed through Appletown. Eli asked one farmer if he would share a small bag of wheat.

"I would like to sow a field of grain in case I am obliged to remain here with the Indians for many years," he told the man. The farmer and his wife talked it over and decided they could spare a quart. "We wish we had more, but we must save some for planting at home."

When the couple left, Eli thanked them. "I will make it go as far as possible," he promised.

That afternoon the Indians brought white prisoners. One was from Minnisink on the Delaware River, two were from Cherry Valley, and a young girl from West Branch. There were more captives that same evening. Eli recognized a widow with two small children, and old Mr. Witherspoon from Wyoming Valley. They were there overnight. The children were whimpering and all were exhausted from their travels. When Eli tried to speak to them it made their Indian captors angry and he was unable to learn anything about his family. The next morning they were gone. Eli felt sorry for them, especially the children.

12

~

For many weeks the daily routine was much the same. Many days Eli took long walks to investigate the surrounding countryside. If, under the right circumstances, there was ever a chance to escape, he wanted to know the lay of the land. He often imagined himself continuing on and simply going home. Eli's heart said "Go", but his mind said, "If you go, you will die." The risk was too great.

Eli was shivering when he joined Sun Spirit as she started food preparations for the day. Due to the cold, he had not slept well. So far, Eli had sustained himself with his belief that the army would surely come soon, and did his best to maintain a remain hopeful.

As he watched Sun Spirit bent over her cook pot, he realized he had genuine affection for her. The old eyes of the ancient woman watched him and he suddenly gave way, crying unashamedly before her. In his hope of rescue, he had not allowed himself to think of the Indians and the coming winter. He could not help it now. He was tired, and felt as helpless as a leaf on a tree waiting for the autumn wind.

"I'm used to wearing more cloths and I've been practically naked all summer. and it's getting cooler every night.," he explained between sobs. "I fear getting sick again. Sun Spirit, what can I do?"

Sun Spirit had noticed how pale Eli appeared.

"Well," Sun Spirit said. "Sukee has been busy sewing a shirt and leggings for you. It was to be a surprise. You must not let on you knew."

"That's wonderful. I won't say a word. I promise."

Eli prayed it would be soon. "Now I know why I haven't seen much of her lately. Thank you, Sun Spirit. You always give me hope."

Eli rubbed his arms, in an effort to get warm. He could hardly wait to see what Sukee created.

As soon as he had carried the water Sun Spirit needed, and completed chores for her, he hurried back to the cave, where he added more grass to his bed. It was warmer there than in the longhouse.

That evening, just before sunset, Cornflower surprised Eli when she arrived at the cave. She carried a colorful wool blanket which she quietly held out to Eli. This was the first time she had approached him since his recovery.

"For you," Cornflower said, handing Eli the gift of a new Indian blanket. After a moments hesitation, but what seemed much longer to Eli, he managed to say, "Thank you Cornflower. I wish I had something to give you in return."

Cornflower blushed pink beneath her light brown complexion, accentuating her lovely features. Eli was so nervous he nearly dropped the blanket he was holding. Without another word, Cornflower quickly turned and ran off like a young doe, her brown legs stepping high over the tall grass.

That night, wrapped in the blanket, Eli slept, but with sleep came strange dreams. First he dreamed of Ruth, then Cornflower. He awoke totally confused. Eli's mind constantly played tricks on him. He wished there was someone with whom he could discuss his dilemma. If only he could go home to his family.

The following morning, when Sukee came, there were dark clouds in the distance and strong winds blowing. She found Eli huddled under Cornflower's blanket, his head covered.

"Good morning Eli. I have a message for you from Sun Spirit. She said to tell you she has much to do and needs her helper."

Eli stuck his head out to see Sukee standing beside him. She was holding a rather large, leather pouch. He was surprised to see her and pretended not to notice what she carried.

"It's so dark I thought it was still night," he said. "What do you have there?" Eli asked, remembering his promise to Sun Spirit.

"I've been concerned about you. With the weather changing it's time you had warm clothing." Sukee smiled as she handed her grandson the shirt and leggings.

Eli was comforted by the feel of the soft deerskin.

"Oh Sukee, there is nothing you could have done to please me more," he said, holding them close. "I am so happy. What a wonderful surprise. Just what I needed, and this pouch is a perfect size. It will hold all my possessions."

It had been extremely difficult for Eli to adjust to living with the Indians, who wore as little as possible except in winter. The young children were completely naked, much of the time. Eli was modest and faced away from Sukee while dressing in his new Indian leggings and shirt. The shirt had a three inch fringe at the bottom and laced up the front with narrow strands of deer skin. The length of the sleeves and legs was just right.

Sukee was pleased to see how well they fit, and thought he looked like an Indian. She hoped, in time, he would see himself as one.

"My grandson deserves the best," Sukee said. "I'm sorry it took so long, but I had to wait for choice hides to make the best for you."

"Thank you, thank you, Sukee. I will wear them with pride, knowing you made them special for me."

Then Eli did something he had not done before, he gave his adopted grandmother a hug of gratitude. Sukee smiled as she returned Eli's hug. It seemed a very natural thing to do.

After Sukee left, Eli stood and admired his new clothe------------s, before folding his blanket and placing it deep inside the cave. Then, he set out to join Sun Spirit, happy with the new day.

On his way, Eli noticed a white man, a stranger, sitting alone by the lake.

"Hello," Eli said, smiling. "Are you lost?"

"No, just resting." he said, looking closely at the white man wearing Indian dress. "Aren't you a white man?" he asked.

"Yes. I was captured in early summer and brought here to Appletown. Where are you from? I keep hoping to meet somebody who can give me news of my family," he said. "I worry about the safety of my wife and children. I hope they are still safe at the fort in Wyoming Valley."

"I'm from west of there, so I can't help you. Sorry. By the way, my name is Samuel Woodward. I'm on my way to preach at a small town church. I've been told it's about a two or three day walk from here."

"I'm pleased to meet you. My name is Eli Jackson."

Since he was fully dressed, Eli felt more comfortable, and was grateful to have another white man to talk to. He was eager to learn whatever he could of the army.

"There have been frequent kidnappings in the last couple months. The Indians must be on the warpath. Perhaps they seek revenge," the preacher told Eli.

Although Eli learned nothing of his family, he and the preacher had a long talk. It turned out they had several things in common. They both liked to read. Both were deeply religious and the Bible was their favorite book.

Before Samuel left early the following morning, he found Eli helping Sun Spirit. "Good morning, Eli. Last night, when I realized you had nothing to read, I decided to give you my Bible. It is old and worn, but I would like you to have it."

Eli protested. "I can't accept it because it would leave you without one. Besides a preacher needs his Bible."

"I can get another one when I reach my destination," he told Eli.

"Well, if you are sure," Eli said. "I would appreciate it. I believe this is the most blessed book in the world, and I will treasure it. Now I can read the Psalms of David. My favorite is, "He leadeth me beside the still waters, He maketh me to lie down in green pastures, He restoreth my soul." Eli quoted and felt blessed.

Thinking of the Psalm reminded him of the situation in which he found himself. His eyes filled with tears as he shook hands and said good bye to the thoughtful and generous man.

Some time later, while on his walk, Eli came upon some Indians who had been hanging meat in trees to dry. Using long tree branches with feathers tied to the ends, the children kept the eagles and hawks away during the day.

One of the men recognized Eli, who stopped to talk.

"What are you doing?" he asked.

"At night we wrap the meat in hides, used only for this purpose. The next morning we uncover them so they can finish drying," he explained.

"That is very interesting," Eli said laughing as he watched the children make a game of keeping the birds away. He sat there for a long time, thinking of his own children. Christmas would be coming in a few months. He wondered where Ruth and the children would be. Had they stayed at the fort, or returned to her parent's home in Connecticut? How he wished he could be with them.

Fawn and Willow saw Eli and hurried to join him, their feathered sticks swinging in all directions as they ran. They giggled as if they had some secret knowledge.

"What are you two up to? Are you not supposed to be chasing birds?"

"Well, we will--soon, if you promise to watch," Fawn told him.

"Not now, but if you are here tomorrow, I will have more time."

"We will come," they both agreed and off they ran.

Because the girls had inquiring, intelligent minds, Sukee had asked Eli to encourage them to speak English. The girls readily absorbed everything. Fawn, the more outgoing, asked many questions about how the white people live.

"Do your children work? What do you do? What are your houses built of? What kind of food do you eat? Do you ride horses?" Questions, questions, questions.

"Wait a minute. Hold it. Slow down."

Eli patiently answered each question while they sat quietly listening. He was surprised when Willow spoke up.

"Can you teach me to mark words on paper like you do?"

"Well now, why would you want to do that?" Eli ask.

"Because, Sukee said you are smart and we should learn from you."

Eli did not know what to say.

"First you will need something to write on and something to write with." Excited, Willow told Eli, "If I had those things I would be able to put words under my pictures."

Eli was impressed and vowed to help this quiet, intelligent girl who reminded him of his daughter, Elizabeth. In the weeks that followed, he acquired paper and pens through Catherine and spent time helping Willow.

Fawn preferred to talk. "I will continue to tell the stories I heard from my elders. I have no need to write."

However, Eli noticed that Fawn looked and listened to what he was teaching Willow. It worked both ways. When Eli inquired about the Indian way of life, the girls were forthcoming in their answers, telling Eli stories that had been passed down from generation to generation.

Eli's children attended school and learned from teachers and books, but he wondered if talking to them about things from the past might be more easily remembered.

Both girls liked to point to objects and have Eli tell them the English name. This also worked both ways. Eli was increasing his knowledge of the Seneca language, which helped him communicate with those Indians who didn't speak English. These activities, along with his work with Sun Spirit, helped Eli pass the time.

Eli observed the way the Indians respected and cared for each other. They protected their families as well as the environment. The Indian's appreciation of the earth paralleled his own ideals as a farmer. He realized more and more how badly the Indians had been abused by white men, and he questioned the behavior of his own people. He better understood why the Indians felt as they did about white men.

~

13

~

Early one morning, while Eli was asleep, he felt something enter the cave and move close to him. Whatever it was settled beside him. He could hear it's regular breathing as it slept. It was the same feeling as, when, on a Sunday afternoon, his old sheep dog came to lay next to him while he took a nap.

Holding his breath, so as not to disturb the creature, Eli slowly turned over. Next to him was a child lying in a fetal position, a leather pouch held tightly in his little hand. His skin was much darker than the Seneca Indians. His short black hair had a purple sheen like that of a raven glowing in the sunlight. He wore only a soiled, ragged cloth wrapped around his waist and his bare feet were crusted with dry mud. As he relaxed, a peaceful smile crossed his face.

Eli didn't know that an old Indian had brought the child to Appletown and directed him to the safe cave to sleep. Eli carefully placed his blanket over the sleeping child, who looked as if he needed more rest. For several hours Eli sat quietly and read his Bible. He often prayed for the safety of the preacher.

About midmorning the boy turned over, stretched and yawned.

"Hello," Eli said.

When there was no reply, Eli said, "I am Eli and pointed to himself. "Who are you? What is your name?"

After rubbing his eyes and looking around, he replied, in clear English. "Little Bear, I'm Little Bear." Then, pointing to Eli, he repeated the name, "Eleee."

"No, Eli. Just Eli."

"Eli–yes?"

"Yes," Eli said. He couldn't help smiling. The boy laughed.

"I was told it was safe for me to sleep here," he explained. "The old man said he had to go find someone named Sukee."

"Come with me," Eli said, offering his hand. "We'll go get something to eat."

"I like you," Little Bear said, smiling up at Eli. I can talk to you because you talk like my mother."

Little Bear had been holding tight to a leather pouch while he slept and continued to hold it as they left the cave and went to see Sun Spirit.

"Where have you been, Eli?" Sun Spirit questioned. "I have been with my friend, Little Bear. He came to visit me last night and we slept late."

Little Bear listened, but remained quiet, never letting go of Eli's hand. Sun Spirit smiled at the small stranger. She noticed how he clung to Eli.

"I bet you're hungry. Would you like to eat with Eli?"

No words were necessary. His smile was sufficient answer. The two sat close as Sun Spirit dished up bowls of hot venison stew. While they ate, Eli revealed what information he had gained from Little Bear.

"Little Bear told me he made the long journey with an old Indian who found him wandering in the woods. His entire village had been burned. Everyone was killed. Because he stayed hidden behind a large rock, he survived."

"I know that fellow," Sun Spirit said. "He's been around these parts for many years. A good man."

Little Bear sat quietly enjoying the hot food. When asked what he carried, Little Bear opened the pouch wide enough for Eli to see the contents. It was full of colorful beads.

"What do you do with them?" Eli ask.

Little Bear drew a simple design in the dirt and proceeded to place different colored beads in a definite pattern. Eli had never seen anything like it.

"It's beautiful," Eli exclaimed. "Where did you learn how to do that?"

Little Bear didn't answer, but in the days that followed he strung beads for the Indian women to use in sewing. Eli was impressed with the work and talked to Sukee about it. Some time later, Sukee acquired a large assortment of glass beads in trade. When she gave them to Little Bear, he couldn't believe they were for him and immediately set to work with renewed energy. Both Eli and Sukee were pleased.

Sukee wondered why Little Bear only communicated with Eli. One day, she was told by a visiter, who had known the child's mother, that Little Bear's mother was English. Her Indian name was Blue Bird because of her bright blue eyes. She had been captured by Indians when she was fifteen. After being forced to take an Indian husband she had given birth to Little Bear.

But she hated the Indians and refused to allow them to be around her son. She kept Little Bear isolated and insisted he speak only English. To keep peace with the others in the tribe, she learned to do beadwork. As a result, Little Bear played with beads and learned the art.

Abigail, Blue Bird's English name, inherited her love of color and design from her artist parents. Using what was available, she created unusual beaded items, gaining the respect of her Indian family. Her son soon learned to chose colored beads, stringing them together in designs of his own.

Eli encouraged Little Bear and, as time passed, the young artist expanded his work. Not only did he continue beadwork for clothing, but he decorated cradle boards, horse gear and other regalia as well. Little Bear's designs were different from those of the Seneca, and became sought after by traders and the Indians from outside Appletown. Eli was pleased with Little Bear's accomplishments. He couldn't have been happier if Little Bear had been his son.

14

~

One day, when Eli was writing in his journal, Little Bear stopped what he was doing and watched Eli write. He drew several rectangles and triangles for Little Bear to see. The boy studied what Eli had done, gave him a big smile and returned to his beads.

Some time later Little Bear presented Eli with the gift of an exquisite bracelet in which he had used large red beads in the shape of triangles, surrounded by small black and yellow rectangles. He had no idea how much the gift meant to Eli, who appreciated the intricate work. It was one of a kind.

"Thank you Little Bear. It's perfect. You've created something very beautiful. It will always remind me of you."

"I made it special for you because you are my friend." A close bond had formed between the two. Little Bear was Eli's shadow, following him everywhere. They had long conversations while walking together. Eli was amazed by all the things he was learning from Little Bear, who knew the names of wild flowers, plants used for medicine and where to find them. Often the boy took hold of Eli's hand as they walked. This both pleased and disturbed Eli because he was constantly reminded him of his children.

One night, when Eli was unable to sleep, he recalled how Little Bear seemed to be drawn to him and wondered if the child was reaching out for a father. Since they were both outsiders, separated from their families, their friendship helped fill the void. After thinking about this, Eli fell into a peaceful sleep.

As more travelers passed through, Eli anxiously waited, longing to see a familiar face. Some were white traders, but most were Indians from other tribes. One individual was Charles James from Virginia. He carried a large knapsack containing fabric, trinkets, and beads to exchange for furs. Charles told Eli the progress the army was making in their effort to move the Indians farther west.

"I believe it's wrong to force the natives to give up their land," the Virginian told Eli.

Eli agreed. "The Indians have lived here for hundreds of years. Why can't they remain? There is certainly enough land in this country for everyone to live in peace."

The two men discussed the situation and both leaned toward support of the Indians. However, knowing they were in the minority, they kept their ideas to themselves.

"I have Indians friends who trust me and I must be careful what I do or say in order to do business with them. You must understand that." "Yes, I do," Eli replied.

Before Charles left, he gave Eli a small harmonica. "Take this. Maybe it will help pass the time, however long you remain here."

"Thank you, Charles. But I have no idea how to play it," Eli said, laughing. "How do you expect me to make music?"

"Oh, you'll be surprised how quickly you'll learn."

Charles laughed as he shook Eli's hand before heading toward the road leading out of Appletown. He wanted to leave before winter weather delayed his trip.

The Indians introduced Eli to another one of their games, Snow Snake. The game was played after the first snowfall and, once again, Eli was invited. It was a favorite winter game of the Indians. Snow snakes were made of smooth, polished, flexible rods of hard wood. They were five to nine feet in length, about one inch in diameter at the head, tapering to half an inch at the tail. When there was enough snow, a shallow course was laid out by pulling a log in a straight line. This packed the snow. The course was then sprinkled with water to form an ice crust. Those playing gathered at one end of the track and took turns throwing the snakes with force, skill and accuracy, so as to make them travel the longest distance in the shortest time.

The purpose of the game was to compare the speed and accuracy of the participant. In spite of having lost two fingers on his right hand to a bear, Tracking Wolf was always the winner.

Hard as he tried, Eli never seemed to get the knack of the game, and Tracking Wolf and the others playfully laughed at his awkward attempts.

15

~

By March, food was scarce. The corn was nearly gone after the long winter. Eli went with the Indians to dig for ground nuts. In March, wood betony sprang up early. They ate it with maple sugar. The Indians were so hungry that, when they found a dead horse, they cooked it and thought it was the best meat in the world. Eli had to agree.

As the days lengthened, the sun warmed the earth. It was time for spring planting. Eli willingly helped the women prepare the soil. This pleased the Indians, especially Sukee and Sun Spirit. Everyone worked hard, knowing that soon fresh food would be available.

Eli watched with interest.

"What are you doing?" he questioned those near him as the Indians proceeded to build mounds.

"First we make a hole in the center of each mound," Cornflower explained. "Then small fresh fish are caught by our men and put into each hole."

She took a few kernels of corn from a pouch she carried and dropped them on top of the fish. Squash seeds were placed in a circle around the corn.

"The squash will grow and help keep the weeds away from the corn," Cornflower told Eli. "Our people have planted the same way for many generations."

Although Sun Spirit was physically unable to work in the garden, she liked to come by to see what the women and Eli were doing.

Eli was impressed. He started to say that when he escaped, he would use the same methods, but instead he said, "Someday I hope the white men will realize what can be learned from the Indians."

In about three weeks, the corn and squash began to grow, and beans were planted. As the cornstalks got higher, the beans climbed up the stocks. There was no need for bean poles. Eli continued to be impressed.

During the spring and summer many people passed through Appletown. Since he was free to go about, he decided to travel with a group of Indian men for a day or two. As they were sharing a meal together before leaving, Eli noticed a young warrior leaning against a tree, watching. The Indian stared at Eli throughout the meal, never changing his grim expression. There was a jagged purple scar across the man's left cheek. Eli felt threatened by the man. Chills ran down his body.

Before they left, Eli told Sukee he didn't expect to be gone long. There seemed to be no hurry and Eli found the Indians company enjoyable. He listened to them discuss what was happening outside of Appletown. About an hour into the walk, Eli was surprised when he suddenly felt a blow to the back of his head, knocking him off balance. Turning, he recognized the scar-faced one, and was struck on the other side of his head, knocking him to the ground. Before anyone noticed what had happened, the Indian disappeared back in the woods.

"What was that all about?" the fellow nearby asked. "I have no idea," Eli replied. "I never saw him before today. The entire time we were eating he glared at me, as if he knew me. I think I'll go back to home," because his head ached, he decided to return to Appletown.

When Sukee saw Eli and the bruises, she said, "You look terrible. What happened to your head?"

After Eli explained and described the scared face, Sukee told him she knew the culprit.

"His name is Man Alone. Three years ago, he was forced to watch his entire family brutally murdered. He has been seeking revenge and has been called Man Alone ever since."

Eli sighed. "The poor fellow," Eli said. "I regret the vicious acts of some white men. However, we are not all bad."

It was getting late as the two walked together under the soft glow of the moonlight, each hoping for peace.

16

~

Around the middle of April, the Indians suddenly changed their behavior toward Eli. It was apparent they were avoiding him. At the same time he was being watched more closely. Whenever he entered the longhouse or approached a group, they became silent. Eli was puzzled by the change and wondered what was wrong.

All day there had been a great deal of activity. While working in the garden, Eli overheard Willow and Fawn whispering to each other. The girls sounded agitated. On hearing the word "Yankee" repeated in their conversation, he listened more closely, but learned nothing. They were usually talkative, but on seeing Eli, they moved further on in the garden.

When Eli looked for Sukee, he found her seated by the lake, her head resting in her hands. Seeing her sitting there, her white braids falling forward and a worried look on her face, Eli became concerned.

"Excuse me," he said, kneeling beside her. "Are you unwell? Is there anything I can do?"

Sukee raised her head slowly and turned a tearstained face toward Eli. "No, my son. The Yankees are coming. Early today our scouts saw soldiers moving this way."

Eager to learn more, but at the same time, not wanting to appear anxious, he sat down next to the woman who had treated him as her own grandson. He wondered if he should ask questions or just remain alert to activities around him? Although Eli was thrilled at the possibility of being rescued by the army, he knew he dare not show his excitement. Lost Arrow stopped to talk to him, and was about to say something, when Cornflower interrupted, which was unlike her. Lost Arrow quickly hurried off toward Sukee's longhouse.

"I'm sorry to trouble you Eli, but I am afraid you might join the soldiers." She was uncertain what she should do and wanted to protect Sukee.

"'I'm concerned for my family, Eli," she said. "My grandmother and Sun Spirit are too old to travel far. We need you to stay here. Willow and Fawn need you too." Then she quietly added, "and I need you."

Cornflower continued. "The Yankee soldiers have taken the Indian town of Onondaga, east of Appletown. They have destroyed houses, burned crops and killed many Indians. Our elders are preparing to move the people twenty miles for a short time, before joining other tribes at Niagara."

"I must talk to your grandmother and find out what she wants me to do, Cornflower. You have all been very kind to me, but I must consider Sukee's wishes. I may not have a choice," he explained before excusing himself and heading to the cave.

Eli quickly gathered his few personal possessions and placed them in a large pouch. If the opportunity presented itself, he would be ready.

All the Indians worked throughout the night, packing necessary equipment. Several young braves were to remain to guard the village.

Early the next morning, Eli and his shadow, Little Bear, accompanied the Indian families. Everyone, including the children, carried clothing, plus extra food for the journey. Little Bear insisted on bringing his precious beads, which was all he could carry. Because Eli had grown close to Little Bear, he felt a sense of responsibility for the child and offered to lighten Little Bear's load by carrying his blanket and clothes.

Progress was slow due to frequent rain showers which made it more difficult for the elderly and the very young. However, the scenery was especially pleasing as they walked the well traveled paths. Buttercups, violets and white and yellow daisies brightened the fields beneath trees, clothed in their bright green leaves.

Because his hands were full, Little Bear was unable to hold Eli's hand as had become his habit, but he managed to walk as close to his friend as possible. Eli couldn't help thinking of his wife and children, as the two walked along together.

After the long, exhausting trip, they arrived at a lake. The town was inhabited by various Indians of the Iroquois Confederation. A few Mohawk and Onondaga Indians were there as well, but the majority were members of Seneca, Oneida and Cayuga tribes. Sukee had once told Eli that the confederation of tribes was known to the French as "Longhouse" and to the English as "Five Nations".

It was evening by the time Sukee's family set up camp in a clearing at the western edge of the town, with other Seneca Indians. After eating some of the food they brought with them, the weary women settled the children for the night, while the men joined a group of other men to learn news of the army. Sukee went to hear what was being said, but she was too tired to stay awake.

The next morning, before the men resumed their talks, Sukee spent time with Eli. Sukee explained, "Seneca women have the power to nominate and veto among their tribe. No child can grow up to be chief unless his mother approves of his candidacy for the position. All descent is through the women and we have the right to select candidates for chief of our clan and tribe from our sons. A mother can even forbid her son to go on the warpath. My grandson was killed by white men, even though he did not choose to fight. I am so glad you are here to take his place, Eli."

After hearing what Sukee had to say, Eli had such a lump in his throat he was unable to utter a word. When he could speak, he managed to thank her for considering him a member of your family.

"I'm proud to be your grandson, Sukee." Although Eli had not chosen to be an Indian, Sukee and her family had been kind and made him feel welcome, so what he said was true.

While the men talked, Eli observed the Indians who had gathered from various tribes to attend the meeting. There were different hairstyles. Some wore their hair tied back in one long braid and others had two braids with pieces of colored fabric woven into them. Most of the young warriors let their hair fall loosely to their shoulders. Many wore headbands with intricate beadwork and designs of animals or pictures of animals carved into the leather. It appeared to Eli that the number of eagle feathers varied and were used mostly by Indian elders.

As Eli watched the activity, Roaring Bear, a stern, dignified Cayuga chief arrived. He was not as tall as the Seneca Indians, who were taller and were known to run faster than other members of the Iroquois nation.

Roaring Bear was one of the tribal leaders who had come to conduct the meeting. He was an impressive figure with his full headdress. He was the only Indian who carried a club.

Roaring Bear had often dealt with white men. He was highly respected by the Iroquois tribes and was influential in decision making concerning the Indians. For this auspicious event he wore a shirt that had once belonged to Tuscarora. It had been a gift to Roaring Bear's father, and was made of the softest doe skin. The sleeves had four inch fringe from elbow to wrist and around the lower edge.

Across the back was a chain of stitches known as, The Covenant Chain, a symbol of peace. One end of the chain was held by a white hand, the other by an Indian. There were five stars representing the Iroquois nations. Below, grouped around the American eagle were thirteen stars for the original colonies. Roaring Bear was proud of the shirt and wore it only for special occasions.

Eli stayed close to Sukee's family, but continued to watch the activities taking place. When he heard the Indian whoop, announcing the arrival of captives, he hurried to see who was there. The Indians brought in two white men whose hands were tied behind their backs. One was a Continental soldier, taken near the town of Wyoming. The other man was young, and had been on his way to join General Sullivan's army. He had blood on his clothes and Eli noticed deep scratches on his face and arms.

The captives were left standing, while the Indians sat and ate bowls of hot stew and corn bread. Meanwhile, the tired, hungry prisoners, expressions of dread on their weary faces, slowly settled themselves on the ground. Much later, their hands were untied and they were given cold leftovers. The soldier was taken away. Eli never saw him again.

Lost Arrow came and took charge of the young captive. He paid no attention to the man's condition, but began questioning him relentlessly about the army's location.

"What is your name?" "I'm Will Scott," he answered. "I took a wrong turn yesterday, while trying to locate the army."

"Where is the army?" "I thought I was getting close, but that's when I was captured, and now I'm not sure where I am," he told Lost Arrow.

"You have not answered my question," Lost Arrow said and he hit the man hard on the side of his head. "Where is the army? What are their plans? You must know something. Why were you out there scouting around alone?"

Somewhat dazed, he looked at his accuser and gave the only answer he had. "The last I heard, General Sullivan had been ordered to continue west and destroy all the Indian towns along the way, taking no prisoners."

Lost Arrow was thoughtful for some time. He looked Will in the eye. "I'll trust you— for now. You will remain here as our prisoner. Try to escape and I will not hesitate to kill you."

Will looked around for the only white man he had seen when he was brought in. At least, he thought the man was white. However, he wondered why the man dressed like an Indian. When he found Eli, he cautiously introduced himself.

"I'm Will Scott," he told Eli. "If you're a white man, why are you wearing Indian clothes?" Eli briefly explained how he had been captured months earlier.

The Indians did not seem to object to the two men talking, and paid little attention to them. After Will had had time to rest, Eli took him to the community cooking area, where Sun Spirit gave them cornbread and buttermilk. The day was warm and pleasant. The two men walked to the lake. As they crossed the meadow, the few cows moved away like shadowed ghosts. The elm trees at the water's edge glowed silver, stirring not a leaf in the still air. Eli was happy to be conversing with another white man and they talked of many things as they walked.

"Do you know of any other captives from Wyoming Valley? My neighbor was taken along with me, but he fought back and may have been killed."

"I wasn't too far from here when the Indians caught me. I don't remember any other captives," Will said. "I had been trying to find the army to enlist, but after the Indians caught me, they took me to some thick briar bushes, stripped me naked, then set several young Indians to whip me through the bushes. Now, no telling what they'll do to me. All I know is that the army is moving rapidly."

"The Indians can be very cruel," Eli told Will. "I was treated badly when I was first captured. I was not sure I would survive. When my captors brought me here, I was given to an old grandmother to replace her grandson. She and her family have treated me very well."

"I'll wash your clothes while you bathe in the creek," Eli said. "You can use my blanket to keep warm while the clothes dry on these warm rocks."

Eli was shocked when he saw how badly Will's body was cut and bruised, especially his feet. As soon as Will was clean, Eli got out a container of medicinal grease Sukee had given him, and carefully applied small amounts to Will's many wounds.

"Thank you, Eli. You have no idea how soothing that feels. What is it? Do you know?"

"I suspect it's bear grease with herbs, but I'm not sure. I've found it useful a number of times."

While they waited for Will's clothes to dry, they ate the apples Sun Spirit had given them. As soon as Will's clothes were dry, he and Eli returned, knowing the Indians were keeping an eye on them.

Eli was sad when, on the following day, the Indians came and told Will he was going to live with his new father and mother in Cayuga. During the brief time Will spent with Eli they had become friends. Eli would miss him.

"Will, remember to behave and not show anger, as my friend Jake did. After living with the Indians, my feelings for them have changed. They care for each other, and value and protect the earth. The Indians believe we are all visitors and no one owns the land. Good luck and God bless you."

Eli was anxious to learn the location of the army, but knew he must be patient. He prayed they would arrive before the Indians moved. Nothing happened in May, and by early June, all the Seneca families had returned to Appletown. Eli had now been captive for a year.

17

~

One day, for a reason known only to the Indians, Eli was left behind in the small hut, where he lived alone for ten days. He was given a cow that produced about a pint of milk a day. He depended on the milk, but sometimes other Indians would milk the cow. There were not enough nuts and edible plants nearby to sustain him. He had no hunting gear. As a result, sometimes Eli went to bed hungry.

One night someone came to the old abandoned cabin where Eli was sleeping. He had heard nothing but was suddenly awakened by a person touching his arm saying, "Cauche gundo", which meant (Come out).

Eli replied, "Este quato", (Go away).

It was too dark for Eli to see the intruder. He was both surprised and terrified. After similar words were said back and forth several times, whoever it was left. He didn't know whether the person was male or female, Indian or white. He was too frightened to go back to sleep. Was it a bad dream, or was it a sign for him to leave? He remembered the way, and at dawn, he set out at to return to Appletown.

When Eli reappeared, the Indians said nothing about why he was left behind. Sukee greeted him with a smile, "I'm glad you're back. There is much work to be done if we are to have a good harvest."

Without further discussion, Eli went to help the women in the garden the remainder of the day. He didn't see Little Bear because he was off by himself making beaded artifacts for Sukee and Cornflower to trade. Eli missed the boy. He felt very lonely. As he toiled, he thought of Will and wondered if he were still alive.

Sukee observed Eli's depression. Since the older men of the tribe were preparing to go fishing, she decided to have Eli join them. Fish were needed and they were plentiful on the other side of the lake.

"Eli, I think you should go fishing with the men today. The weather is perfect. Besides, it will do you good."

He didn't really feel like it, but to please Sukee, he agreed to go. Eli had always enjoyed fishing on the Susquehanna River back home, but today, thinking about it made him homesick.

They crossed the lake in two large birchbark canoes, and set up where they would spend the day. Before sunset, as the men were packing the fish for the return trip, Eli caught a large fish. It was more than twice the size of any the Indians had in either canoe. They praised Eli.

"Our earth mother favors you today." they told him.

It was the biggest, best fish the Indians had seen for a very long time.

As the fish was unloaded, the men held Eli's large fish for Sukee to see. "Eli is a good fisherman," they told her.

Sukee asked if Eli's fish might go to Sun Spirit for their next meal. When they agreed, she was very excited and happy. Eli felt ashamed for not being more grateful for all Sukee had done for him.

One morning, before dawn, an exhausted, bent figure staggered out of the woods and fell near the door of Sukee's longhouse. Sukee had been having strange dreams when she found herself suddenly awake. She got out of bed and wandered over to the door, where she yawned and stretched as she gazed at a full moon on the horizon. When she looked down, Sukee saw what seemed to be a pile of rags that wasn't there the night before. As she approached, she saw that it was an elderly Indian woman who didn't appear to be breathing.

Stooping beside the prostate figure, Sukee gently touched the woman's cold hand saying, "Hello! Hello! Who are you?"

The ragged bundle moved ever so slightly and whispered, "Brr, brr."

The stranger's torn, dirty and rumpled clothing reeked of stale sweat and smoke. The wrinkled skin on her sharp features was pale and had patches of what looked to Sukee like soot.

Meanwhile, Cornflower awoke and wondered why her grandmother was up so early, and who she was talking to at this hour. Outside, she found Sukee leaning over what she thought was a lifeless body of a child. She proceeded to light some kindling in the nearby fire pit and hung a kettle of broth to heat, while Sukee went inside for warm blankets and clean rags. After Sukee and Cornflower removed the woman's filthy clothes, they carefully bathed the frail woman and wrapped her against the morning chill. Then they placed her on a fur pelt, covering her with a second blanket.

Cornflower gently held the patient's head, while Sukee encouraged her to take small sips of the hot broth. "Brr, brr," the stranger repeated as she slowly swallowed the nourishing liquid. When it was gone, the exhausted woman fell back on the thick pelts and was instantly asleep.

At first light, other members of Sukee's family began to come out to see who was there. Fawn and Willow were especially curious as they approached, rubbing their sleepy eyes. Little Bear, who usually slept later, soon joined them.

When Little Bear saw the old woman lying before him, he called out, "Mintaka, Mintaka," and quickly dropped to his knees and embraced her. Tears flowed from his big dark eyes. "Mintaka, speak to me," he pleaded.

"How did you find me? How did you get here?"

The only response was her soft breathing. Seeing Little Bear's reaction, Sukee asked, "Who is she? Who is this woman?" "She's my grandmother. I thought she was dead, that she was killed with all the others!"

The old woman continued to sleep while Little Bear stayed at her side, holding her hand and whispering comforting, loving words. Sukee and members of her family stayed close. Little Bear talked more than any time since his arrival in Appletown. He told them he didn't remember his father, and that his mother was killed by white soldiers.

"My grandmother, Mintaka, took me to her village to live with her. She gave me more beads to finish some of the things my mother had taught me. Mintaka has many grandchildren. She said I was the only one who liked to work with beads."

"The great spirit has given you a special gift. Use it wisely," she told me. "I love my Mintaka and wanted to please her." Little Bear seemed to relax as he continued to tell of his life.

"When I watched the soldiers burn our village, I was alone and hid behind a big rock so they didn't see me. I was very afraid and stayed there all night. The next morning I gathered my beads and ran. I ran and ran until my side hurt so much I crawled behind a dead tree that had fallen and slept. I was still asleep when a stranger found me.

"It's alright," he told me. He said he would not harm me and asked where I was going. When I said I had no place to go, he brought me here to his friend Sukee."

Eli had joined the group and had sat nearby listening. He was amazed. He had never heard Little Bear talk so much.

Now it seemed Little Bear could not stop talking. Hearing Little Bear's story made Eli sad. He was lonely and missed his family more each day.

Little Bear continued, "Mintaka's husband, my grandfather, was from a Seneca tribe. It is Indian law that when a man marries someone from another tribe, he must live with the woman's people. My grandfather was a respected elder for many years until he died of the white man's sickness."

Mintaka awoke late that afternoon. When she saw her grandson, she tried to raise her head to see him better. She squinted and looked at Little Bear in disbelief.

"Brr, Brr, my Bear, is it really you?" she said, as she reached to hug Little Bear. "When I couldn't find you, I thought the soldiers had taken you. I was in the cave and stayed there 'til I felt it was safe to come out. All the people in our village are dead."

Mintaka had traveled many miles. Along the way she had inquired of other Indians, asking if they had seen any survivors of her clan. One day, her spirits were lifted when a young girl told of seeing an Indian boy traveling with an old man. The child described Little Bear and said he carried beads. Mintaka had renewed hope. She forced herself to go on in the direction the girl indicated. She rested where she felt safe, for fear of being caught and killed.

Mintaka was disoriented, undernourished and very, very tired from her ordeal.

Little Bear did his best to explain to his grandmother how a man found him and brought him to Sukee's village. Drawing her closer to Mintaka, Little Bear placed Sukee's warm hand on Mintaka's thin, cold one.

"Sukee is my new mother," he said to Mintaka. "She is good to me. I make things with beads, like you taught me. Sukee and Cornflower use them to trade or sell."

Then Little Bear reached out to Eli and brought him closer to Mintaka.

"Eli is my friend," he explained. "He is not a bad white man. His family is far away. He is like a father to Little Bear."

Mintaka smiled gently at her grandson. He knew she understood.

In the weeks that followed, Mintaka ate, rested and regained some of her strength. She and Sukee spent much time together, which pleased Little Bear because both women were special to him.

Mintaka appeared to be doing well when, late one night, she awoke and lay very still. In a weak voice, she whispered an old Indian prayer. She asked the Great Spirit to give her strength and wisdom.

In the morning, when Little Bear went to greet Mintaka, she did not respond. He feared she had died and ran to find Sukee.

Sukee came and looked at Mintaka.

"Your grandmother is in a very deep sleep," she told Little Bear, placing her arm around the child. "She awaits release from this world before tra--veling on her final journey. Mintaka is tired. See how peaceful she looks. You wait here beside her. I'll be back soon," and Sukee hurried off.

When she returned, many members of the tribe followed quietly. They formed a circle around Mintaka and, in unison, spoke in their native language;

"We let you go. Go to the light. We love you. Find the light." One by one, they recited the words of the old prayer Mintaka had said earlier. These words were broken by chanting, until, finally Mintaka was silent forever.

18

~

Little Bear had witnessed similar ceremonies, but this one brought reality closer to him. He fought back tears and tried hard to be brave, as Mintaka had taught him.

Eli was at the lake when Mintaka died. He had been struggling for several days with a plan to escape. After learning that the army was progressing in the direction of Appletown, he thought that maybe, if he were able to intercept the troops, he could lead them away from Appletown and his Indian family. He hadn't forgotten Lost Arrow's threat to kill him if he tried to escape and wondered if, since they had become friends, Lost Arrow would still carry out the threat.

Sukee could trust Eli, and told Eli he might use one of the horses, as long as he didn't stray too far. They were kept in a corral where two or three Indians kept watch. The mare Eli usually rode was standing near the entrance, and only one guard was on duty. He had no way of knowing that the other two were honoring Little Bear's grandmother by attending the special ceremony for her. A light rain fell as Eli mounted and rode slowly so as not to attract attention. He rode past a rundown split rail fence, a row of stately maple trees, thick blackberry bushes and what looked like the remains of an old stone chimney. He wondered if the property had belonged to a settler at one time.

The horse plodded along while Eli's mind drifted. He wondered what Ruth was doing. Were she and the children well? He missed them so much, and wanted desperately to go home. He felt as old as the rocks that lined the path. He prayed for his family and hoped he was doing the right thing in trying to escape.

As he rounded a curve, an elderly Indian stepped out from behind the trees and signaled for Eli to halt.

"Are you Eli?" the man asked in good English.

Eli said, "Why do you want to know?"

"I am Walking Eagle. Sukee is my wife."

Eli got off his horse and stood next to it.

"I'm Eli. Sukee has told me about you. What do you want of me? Can I help you?" "Yes, I would like you to go with me to collect salt at the spring. We can get acquainted on the way. Let the horse go. She will find her own way home."

Since Walking Eagle seemed to pose no threat, Eli removed the bag containing his pouch from the horse, slapped the horse's rump, and sent it trotting off. A light rain fell on the two, as they walked single file, Eli following------------*+ Walking Eagle.

"Why are you called Walking Eagle?" Eli asked. Walking Eagle explained as they continued in the direction of the spring. "I was born during a big snow storm. After I was born, my mother looked outside and saw an eagle walking in the snow and named me Walking Eagle."

In good English, Walking Eagle said, "Sukee has been my wife for a long time. She is a very intelligent, hard working woman. We grew up in different tribes. When we were young and attended a pow-wow, I saw her watching me. One day she informed me I was to be her husband. Well, that was fine, until she said I had to learn to speak the white man's talk, but by then I wanted her, too. What could I do?"

A spark of mischief glimmered in his dark, old eyes and a big grin covered his wrinkled face. Walking Eagle hesitated for a moment as he watched for Eli's reaction.

"A white friend of French Catherine taught me your language."

Eli couldn't help liking the man. He had to laugh at the Indian's story. He knew Sukee was married, but had never met this charming fellow. Eli found himself wanting to help Walking Eagle in whatever way he could.

The showers stopped, but the day remained hot and humid. Both men were wearing loincloths, and for once, Eli was glad. Walking Eagle was easy to know. As soon as they reached the salt spring, a fire was built and a kettle was filled with water from the spring. Only after it was built did they take time to eat. Corn bread and a few apples was all Eli had brought with him. He had planned to catch fish along the way.

Walking Eagle shared some dried venison while they waited, as steam drifted from the boiling pot. Eli was impressed by how quickly the unsaturated salt was developing. The procedure was repeated many times as they added more water, and collected enough wood to keep the fire burning. The smoke from the fire kept the mosquitos away.

Finally, Walking Eagle told Eli, "We have enough salt to share." "This salt is the best I've ever tasted," Eli said.

Having no choice, he agreed to help Walking Eagle deliver the salt. Each man carried two bags that seemed to get heavier as the hours passed. It was nearly dark when they stopped for the night. Eli gathered wood and built a fire, while Walking Eagle went in search of food. When he returned with two rabbits, he quickly skinned them and secured each animal to a strong stick, ready to hang over the hot fire. Just then two Indian families approached from the opposite direction. There were six adults and five children.

"They look as tired as we are," Walking Eagle said to Eli, as the old Indian stepped forward to greet the newcomers.

That night they all camped together, sharing what food they had. The men smoked and talked, while the women and children retired. Eli settled himself a short distance away and fell into an exhausted sleep thinking about his failed escape.

Well before dawn, four of the Indian men took up their bows, arrows, knifes and quietly left. Eli saw them go, but paid no attention, since he felt safe with Walking Eagle asleep beside him.

About sunrise, when the people began to stir, a young bull appeared, followed by the four Indians. They had stolen it from a pasture where they had seen it the previous day. They said it was easier to walk the animal, rather than kill it first and have to carry it.

Eli was amazed at how fast the Indians set to work. They quickly cut the bull's throat and drank the fresh blood. After the skin was removed, the women proceeded to cut the meat into various sized chunks. The heart, liver and blood, considered delicacies, were shared in what appeared to Eli some kind of special ceremony. However, Eli declined to partake. He was anxious to continue with his escape plan.

In ten days, the entire animal was consumed. Walking Eagle was enjoying time with the other Indians and was in no hurry to leave. They caught eels and muskrats to eat and felt they were living exceedingly well. When, a week later another Indian family showed up with a horse they had killed, it too was cooked and eaten. No one seemed to care what day it was, and all but Eli were content to stay.

"I think it's time to deliver the salt," Walking Eagle finally announced.

Eli was only too happy to move on. He was surprised when Walking Eagle shared the salt they had collected, acquired a canoe and agreed to take Eli about ten miles, where he was left him to go his own way. Carrying his few belongings and the salt, he walked most of the day. He was surprised to be going off alone and couldn't believe his good fortune. When he found a head from a horse that had been recently killed, he tore off what meat he could and carried it with him.

After Eli grew tired, he left the salt in an abandoned hut, where he rested before catching a horse that was wandering nearby. He rode and rode for several hours. Fearing he might meet Indians, he left the horse and continued on foot. Eli had been gone for three weeks, with no sign of the army. He decided to return to Appletown.

19

~

Sukee was happy to see Eli. She knew he had been at the salt spring with Walking Eagle and gave him what the Seneca call, "Benjamin's Mess" a kind of feast. Eli wondered if Sukee had suspected he was planning to escape and was celebrating the fact that he returned on his own. Many neighbors joined in the party, bringing food and expressing their joy at his return. Cornflower never let him out of her sight, but stayed were she could view all the activity, maintaining a secure boundary between herself and Eli. She wore colorful wild flowers braided in her long hair. Eli thought she looked beautiful, but paid her no special attention.

Before nightfall, word came that the army was fast approaching. Eli was troubled. He hoped to escape, but hated the thought of his Indian family being threatened. Once again he reasoned that, if he were to succeed in connecting with the army, he could lead the troops away from Appletown and afterwards eventually return home.

When Eli mentioned that he'd left a bag of salt at the old house, the Indians became excited and furnished a horse so he could retrieve the salt. This gave the Indians another reason to celebrate, and the feasting continued on into the night. Produce from their garden was plentiful. Everyone was happy as they ate, and danced to the beat of the drums.

After making the decision to attempt another escape, Eli set out on his early morning walk to the lake. He was nervous and had butterflies in his stomach as he entered the cave. As he reached for his pouch and the blanket Cornflower had given him, he thought he detected movement in the tall grass near the cave's entrance.

"Who's there?" he asked. The grass parted as Little Bear slowly appeared from his hiding place. "It's me," Little Bear whispered. "What are you doing? I saw you leave the longhouse, and I need to talk to you."

"Oh Little Bear, you should not have come," Eli scolded. "I couldn't stand the thought of leaving you, but I have to find the army and return to my wife and children. It's very important that you stay here with Sukee. She loves you and will care for you and see that you get a good education. Your grandmother wanted that for you."

Little Bear stood very still looking at Eli in disbelief. Eli softened his approach. "Please, try to understand. I miss my other family very much. If they are still alive, I need to go back and take care of them. You belong here with the Indians. Our lives are entirely different. If the soldiers find me living with the Indians, they will kill me."

"Can I go with you? I can be your son too," Little Bear coaxed as he struggled to keep from crying. The pain on the child's face nearly broke Eli's heart. He had come to love Little Bear since the day he arrived in Appletown, a lost, lonely, quiet child. This was one of the most difficult things Eli had ever had to do. Kneeling, he took Little Bear in his arms and held him.

"Mintaka traveled a very long way and died peacefully, knowing you were safe with Sukee. Now you have a new Indian family that loves you. Once you told me that your grandfather taught you to be a good and brave Indian. Show Sukee and the others that you can grow up to be a fine, brave man. I love you as my own son and will always be your friend. One day, when the war is over, I hope to come back."

As Little Bear brushed his tears away. He stood as a breeze rustled the leaves in a whisper. Suddenly alert, Little Bear listened carefully. "Hear the trees," he said to Eli. "They are telling us it is alright. It is time for you to go. I will tell no one." Startled, Eli gave Little Bear a final embrace. Little Bear quickly turned, looking forward, head held high as he headed home without looking back.

Since it was nearly noon Eli stayed in the cave and tried to rest. He would leave after dark. No need to be seen if he could avoid it. He waited as long as he could and then, very slowly and quietly, Eli crept outside. No one in sight. Good. The horse corral was on the other side of a small hill, between the cave and the village. Lying nearby on his stomach, Eli waited, his heart beating wildly, and listened. Except for the occasional movement and breathing of the horses, all was quiet. Inch by inch Eli slowly crept to the top of the hill where he could see. The full moon made it possible to see each animal. He recognized a dark mare he had used when accompanying the Indians.

The Indian guard was on the far side, away from where Eli approached. The man's chin rested on his chest and he appeared to be very relaxed. When a cloud partially blocked the moon, Eli stood and, taking one careful step at a time, he reached a large tree next to the horses and inched himself close enough to whisper to the horse and calmly stroke it's head and neck.

After cutting the single rope that surrounded the corral, he led the horse away and hoped the sound of his pounding heart would not wake the guard. Praying with every step, Eli led the animal toward a familiar trail through the woods, walking the horse before mounting. Then he urged the horse to run at top speed, covering as many miles as possible before dawn. Fearing being seen in daylight, he took a less traveled path.

That evening, tired after a long, hard ride, the horse was hobbled where grass was plentiful, while Eli tried to sleep. The smallest sound disturbed him. A twig snapping, a leaf fluttering to the ground, even the wind in the trees made Eli alert to possible danger. He was glad he had learned to listen like an Indian. When he was able to, Eli moved to a place where the horse could drink and he could fish.

A few elderly Indians lived nearby. They were friendly and, having seen Eli many times, they paid no attention. One of the women gave him enough apples to share with his horse. This place had felt peaceful in the past. A fast flowing stream passed through the heavily wooded area. A cool breeze, combined with the sound of the water rippling over the rocks, added to the serenity. He was reminded of a place he fished as a child, calling him home. Eli found himself relaxing, and fell asleep before he had time to fish.

20

~

When he awoke, he looked around at the tall trees and blue sky and contemplated his surroundings more closely as he mulled over the events leading him here. Eli appreciated having been born and raised in the country. Since living with the Indians and learning their ways, he had a greater admiration for them and their quality of life and respect for the land. It was almost spiritual. Everything around him was alive with it's own special energy. He vowed that, if he succeeded to return home, he would teach his children to respect the earth and all things in nature.

While fishing from the bank, Eli questioned the situation in which he found himself. He thanked God for this quiet time. He was concerned about his family and was thinking about them and praying for courage to continue his escape. He didn't notice the arrival of an old woman until she quietly lowered herself a few feet away.

"Hello", Eli said, turning to face her. She spoke so softly Eli was unable to hear her. "What is it? Are you alright?" Eli asked. She smiled and spoke to Eli in a such a soft voice, it was difficult for Eli to hear or understand.

Her clothes were well worn but clean. Her dark eyes were alert to her surroundings. High cheekbones dominated her wrinkled face. Her grey hair was neatly braided.

Speaking a little louder, she said, “My name Mary. Old Joe say you good man. Work hard. Hoe corn too much work. Me too old. You hoe, I give you venison.” Having no idea how long before he might meet the army, Eli considered her offer.

After introducing himself, Eli he asked, “How much meat will you give me? Where is your cornfield?” She stood slowly and pointed. “Over there. Not far. I give you plenty food.”

Eli agreed, and followed her to a field a short distance away, where he spent the rest of the day hoeing corn. Mary came to Eli. “Sleep here,” she offered, nodding her head in the direction of her small house. “My husband dead long time.”

Her dark old eyes looked sad at the memory. Eli was touched by the kindness of this frail women who lived alone, and agreed to wait ‘til the next day to leave. Mary shared her simple evening meal of fresh baked bread, eggs, fruit and vegetables with Eli before retiring.

The following morning, Eli was given a generous supply of venison as promised, and a bag of apples she had picked from one of her trees.

“This was my husband’s rifle,” Mary said as she held it out to Eli. “My man use,” she said. “Now, you take.” “I can’t ,” Eli said. “You live here alone and need it for protection.”

“You take, please,” she insisted. “I no need. Never use.” She handed the big gun to Eli, along with what ammunition she had. Mary smiled as if she had accomplished a very important mission. She seemed happy to have something to give Eli.

Feeling fortunate to have a weapon Eli felt some of his prayers had been answered. The venison, along with any fish he caught, would help him survive for days.

By noon he realized he was in unfamiliar territory and was unsure which direction to travel. The creek he'd been following divided into two separate steams. The forest was thicker. Nothing looked as he remembered. The narrow path had frequent holes made by rodents. Fearing the horse might step in one, he got off and led the horse until the trail became wider.

While walking, Eli thought of his own horses and wished he were back home tending to his farm animals. By mid-afternoon, it was so hot he stopped in the shade along the bank, where both he and the horse enjoyed a cool drink. He planned to take a short rest before moving on, but instead he fell asleep, until he heard the horse whinny.

Eli carefully reached for the loaded rifle. As he did so he spotted a large rattlesnake by a rock in the sun, about half way between him and the horse. The snake lay coiled, it's head raised ready to strike. Eli's heart sounded like Indian drums. He remained perfectly still, holding his breath. Once, having seen a horse suffer after being bitten, Eli hoped he was not about to see it happen again.

Swish! Eli felt the air move near his right shoulder. The rattler's head split open as it's body uncoiled and squirmed in the dust. Eli let out his breath. An Indian youth stood about twelve feet away, bow in hand. The Indian greeted Eli with a friendly smile as he came forward. He retrieved the arrow he'd used to kill the snake before sitting across from Eli. He placed it with the rest of his arrows on the ground next to his bow before accepting an apple Eli offered.

Without a word, Eli walked over and spoke softly to the horse as he stroked the animal tenderly. "I see you care about animals. I respect you for that. There are many white men who abuse them," the young man said.

"Thank you for saving us. That snake would have bitten either me or the horse."

"If you have no use for the snake I would like to have it."

When Eli nodded in agreement, knowing the Indians ate the meat and used the skins, the young man placed the reptile in his sack.

"Beware, there are things far worse than snakes the way you are going, I see a dark trail ahead of you," he said eating the apple as he walked away. Eli was superstitious about some of the Indian's spiritual beliefs and decided to return to Appeltown.

The sky was overcast as he picked his way over fallen tree trunks at a slow pace. Disheartened at his second attempt to escape, he was in no hurry.

21

~

Eli was remembering life on his farm as he trudged slowly along the the narrow dirt road. He was remembering how his wife and young son had cleared trees from the land. They used them to build a sturdy house. With Ruth at his side, the farm had supported his family--until the Indian raids. Along with their neighbors, Eli and his family had moved to the safety of the fort. Living in close quarters had been a challenge. If the raids became less frequent, they hoped to return home.

The horse now knew the way, making it easier for Eli's thoughts to wander. Here he was, living in a different kind of country, feeling at ease in his surroundings since his capture, in a place that provided for all his needs. Food, shelter, warm clothes, pure fresh water were readily available and yes, even serenity. Perhaps he should settle for this and willingly accept life with the Indians. They had taught him much about life and survival.

Eli realized he had grown more cognizant of his surroundings. The deep tracks of a bear, the distinctive footprints of deer, weasel, fox and other wild animals. He had learned to identify many different bird calls and heard several coming from the trees overhead.

Eli wondered if he was being hasty in leaving his present home? Should he stay here, take an Indian wife and start another family? His feelings were so strong, so intense he was alarmed. What was he thinking? It occurred to him that Cornflower had been in his recent dreams. She was young and beautiful. However, he certainly couldn't blame her if she thought him too old or not as attractive as one of the young Indian braves.

Eli was both emotionally and physically exhausted. Why did life have to be so complicated? He compared life on the farmland he owned to the way the Indians lived off the land but owned none. All Indians helped raise the tribe's children. The white families each raised their own. Each loved their children equally. There were things he liked about both ways of life.

He had been married to Ruth for seventeen years and prayed she would forgive him. It seemed ages since he and Jake set out for the grist mill. He could still see Ruth's brave smile, as she waved on that fateful day.

Continuing to quietly observe those around him he saw that they were simple people with great respect for Mother Earth. They believed the Great Spirit would always provide for them and protect them.

As he traveled, Eli liked to think about how Sun Spirit made boiled corn bread. First she mixed enough boiling water to make a thick paste, then she added whatever berries available; currant, raisin, strawberry, elderberry, blackberry or huckleberry. Sometimes she stirred walnut or butternut meats into the dough. A four inch ball of dough was patted down to about one and a half inches across, then carefully slid into a kettle of boiling water and allowed to boil until the bread floated, about one hour.

The liquid in which the bread was boiled was thickened with course corn meal. Either maple syrup, or salt and meat drippings were added. This was sopped up with the corn bread.

Eli especially liked the aroma when Sun Spirit added the fragrant berries. The warm liquid soothed his throat and the savory bread satisfied his hunger. If he escaped he'd never again see Sun Spirit's strong brown hands stir the dough.

He remembered eating boiled cornbread samples Sun Spirit had given him. Eli had thanked her as he wiped the crumbs from the corner of his mouth. He had grinned when Sun Spirit handed him a second piece. He smiled now, as he recalled the intense flavor of blueberries in the bread. He was hungry, and wished he had some now.

And his thoughts turned, once again, to Cornflower. If he left, Cornflower's dark eyes would not be there to warm his heart. Could he leave this all behind? He decided to decide later. With that thought, his mind cleared, the tension ebbed away.

The shadows were growing long across the path. Eli regretted it would be too late to reach home tonight. Tomorrow when he reached Appletown, would Cornflower be glad to see him?

22

~

The early morning fragrance of pines filled Eli with pleasant thoughts as he started the day. It was nearly noon before the trees thinned and streaks of light filtered through. As he reached a fork in the path he heard a sharp whistle, and turned to see Walking Eagle running toward him. A happy grin covering the old Indian's weathered features as he greeted Eli.

"I believe we have the same destination," he said. "We need to talk."

The two walked side by side. Eli listened, as Walking Eagle told stories about his ancestors. He suddenly realized the subject had changed, it was now about him.

"Sukee and I both like and respect you. She says you have become an Indian, a good Indian since joining our family. We feel it is time for you to take a wife."

Eli was too surprised to respond. His decision would affect the future of his life with the Indians. "I will consider what you have said, Walking Eagle. You may be right."

He would think about it. Cornflower was the only woman who came to mind. Would she agree to be his wife? Having spent many long, lonely days since his capture, was it time to think about staying?

Sukee and Cornflower had been very kind to him. They had nursed him when he was very ill. He remembered the warm blanket Cornflower had given him, and the clothes she and Sukee had made for him.

Eli also missed Little Bear, as well as other family members, and pondered these things as Walking Eagle continued to enlighten him.

"You must talk to Sukee soon. She will know what must be done."

All this time Eli had tried to assimilate what Walking Eagle was telling him, and was relieved when a group of Indians, traveling in the same direction, asked to join them.

"There are many miles yet to travel. It we share what food we have it will be easier. There will be more men to hunt and fish, while the women cook," Walking Eagle explained.

"A good idea," Eli said, agreeing to go along with Walking Eagle.

The Indians never seemed to be in any hurry. This troubled Eli, because he was anxious to talk to Sukee. Unable to make a decision, he hoped Sukee could answer some questions that troubled him.

As soon as they arrived in Appletown, Sukee rushed to meet them. She acknowledged her husband and then quickly turned her attention to Eli. She took him in her strong arms and he thought she would never let him go.

When she released Eli, she said. "I'm happy to have you here. When I sent Walking Eagle to find you I wasn't sure you would come back to us. Now that you have, my hopes are that you will agree to stay."

Cornflower stood in the shadows where she could see but not be seen. She trembled, knowing of Sukee's plans to ask Eli to be her husband.

The first chance he got, Eli went in search of Cornflower and found her in the garden, gathering corn and beans. She stood straight and tall, with her back to him after placing the last squash in her large basket. She looked so beautiful, with her shiny black hair falling to her waist. Her strong brown arms held the basket close as she turned and walked in the direction where Eli was standing. He thought she would make a lovely painting, with the late afternoon sun behind her.

Eli stepped forward. "Hello, I've been looking for you." He reached for the basket, but Cornflower refused to let him carry it. That was a woman's duty. They walked in the the direction of the longhouse.

Eli smiled. "We need to talk. Do you have time to fix some food and go spend some time together at the lake?

Cornflower gave Eli a shy smile and proceeded to take the vegetables to where Sukee waited. Not knowing what to expect, he sat on the bench by Sukee's door, surprised at how strong his emotions were where Cornflower was concerned. He was aware of the strong feelings stirring inside him. He was about to leave when she hurried toward him, carrying a food basket. She wore a colorful shawl around her shoulders. Flames of orange and purple filtered into deeper tones of aqua and midnight blue across her otherwise somber clothes.

"I must return by sundown," she cheerfully announced.

It was already late afternoon. They wouldn't have much time. "That's fine," Eli happily replied.

They steeped out into a landscape washed with watercolors of gray, yellow and brown, smeared with wide brush strokes as the sun appeared lower on the horizon. Eli was happy as he led the way along a narrow pathway following a stream leading to the lake.

Time passed quickly, while Eli and Cornflower ate the apples and drank buttermilk. They sat quietly together, neither one able to say what was on their mind.

Cornflower told Eli, "My family is happy you came home. The tribe is having a feast in your honor. We must join them." Eli quietly followed Cornflower back the way they had come.

The celebration of Eli's return was in progress. The Indians danced and sang and enjoyed the special food prepared by Sun Spirit for the occasion. Fresh venison, smoked fish, flatbread and fruit were plentiful. Cornflower served Eli, unlike previous times. She then served herself and sat beside Eli. Even though not much was said between them, Eli felt content.

Close to midnight the celebration came to a sudden halt when scouts reported news of soldiers fast approaching a village east of Appletown. The Indians hurried their families inside and the men discussed what action was to be taken.

Swift Arrow and Sukee were talking, all the while looking in Eli's direction. Eli said to himself, "I'm too tired to worry about it tonight," and went to bed where he thought about Ruth and his children. What would become of them? Finally he fell into a restless sleep and dreamed of both families--very confusing and disturbing. He dreamed of Cornflower and Ruth. They were together, simply sitting near each other. There were many children present, running around making loud noises. He awoke with a headache and wondered what the dream meant.

23

~

Early in the morning Sukee came to him.

"Eli, wake up, wake up." Slowly rubbing his eyes he squinted to see her standing in the doorway.

"What is it, Sukee? It isn't even daylight. Is something wrong?"

Sukee entered and sat on the edge of Eli's bed.

"Overnight the army has moved closer. We feel it is urgent that you take an Indian wife as soon as possible. There is very little time. By marrying an Indian, you will become a full member of our tribe."

Eli was fully awake and quickly sat up. "Who am I to marry?"

"Cornflower, of course. She loves you, and her grandfather and I would be happy to have you as a full grandson, not simply adopted."

Sukee silently pleaded with her eyes. Eli felt her love and had come to love her. How could he turn her down at such a serious moment? Walking Eagle quickly joined them.

"Is he ready? I have made all the arrangements. Can we proceed with the ceremony?" he asked.

Anxiously awaiting Eli's response, Sukee held her breath. When the answer finally came, the wrinkles in Sukee's old face softened and her eyes brightened with relief.

"I agree to wed Cornflower, but there is one condition," Eli said. "She must also agree."

Sukee smiled. "I will go to my granddaughter and give her the good news. She has always been very shy, but you must know she has loved you since the day Lost Arrow brought you to live with us. The ceremony will take place later today. Be ready to join us when Walking Eagle comes for you."

Eli needed to spend some time alone, and retreated to a small secluded inlet. He prayed for courage, while bathing in the cool refreshing water. After drying himself in the warm breeze under the tall pines, Eli dressed in the leggings and tunic Sukee and Cornflower had made for him before sitting in quiet meditation.

Eli prayed. "Lord, please help me make the right decision. I seems that I'm destined to remain here with the Indians. I have been unable to escape in all this time. If it is your will that I marry Cornflower, give me some sign. Whatever happens, please keep Ruth and the children safe. Amen."

Emotionally spent, Eli lay back looking at the clouds high above the trees. Thinking he was alone, he suddenly sensed movement nearby and was surprised to hear Lost Arrow's voice.

"I've been looking for you, Eli. I heard about your wedding. You will be welcome in our tribe. You will soon become my brother. However, before you take Cornflower as your bride you must be cleansed."

Eli had just finished bathing but, rather than argue, he followed Lost Arrow to a place he had passed many times. "We call this the Hot Rock Sweat Lodge," Lost Arrow explained as they approached.

Eli followed his friend into the large mound. The structure was built on a circular base. Willow shoots were planted like interlocking croquet wickets to make a frame. Where the ribs crossed they were tied together with strips of bark. The frame was covered with reed mats topped with hides.

A round pit had been dug in the center. Lost Arrow entered the lodge which faced east, in a clockwise direction.

"Follow me, Eli," Lost Arrow said, after he had placed rocks (which had been heating outside) into the lodge. The door flap was closed and the interior heated up like a sauna.

A ceremony, which took place inside, consisted of four rounds of prayers, spiritual songs and drumming. As the men prayed, Lost Arrow threw water on the heated rocks. Sweet grass was burned. Eli was not accustomed to the smoke. It made him sick to his stomach. Soaked with sweat he felt light headed and relaxed. At this point in time he no longer cared what happened.

After the ceremony was finished, they exited and lay on the grass to cool their bodies. Eli turned to Lost Arrow who lay near him.

"I feel like a newborn baby," he said. "The sweat lodge has spiritual powers. It rids the body of evil spirits, cleanses and purges the body."

"Here, Eli, take these," Lost Arrow said, handed him several soft fir boughs. "Rub your body with them. They will give your body power and scent. Most of us sweat longer, but this was your first time, so that was enough."

Knowing he was being prepared for his wedding, Eli did as he was told. "I think I'm as clean as I will ever be," he told Lost Arrow.

"You have done well. Walking Eagle and Sukee will be pleased."

All the stones were saved and piled outside the sweat lodge, where they would remain undisturbed. An Indian would not think of desecrating them in any way.

"Come with me, Eli, We always follow the sweat with a dip in the stream," he explained as they walked to the creek.

After Eli got out of the water and was dry, Lost Arrow presented him with new deerskin shirt and leggings. The silver broach, given to him by Sukee months earlier, was fastened to the shirt.

"You must look as much like an Indian as possible."

As a final touch Lost Arrow placed a deerskin headband around Eli's head. It had one eagle feather pointing toward the ground, a sign of peace.

Seeing his reflection in the water, Eli was surprised. Maybe he could pass as an Indian in spite of the fact that most of the Indians were much taller. He was in the prime of his life, a ruggedly handsome man. His dark hair, now shoulder length, had many streaks of grey that were not there when he was captured. His skin had darkened from hours spent in the sun, but his blue eyes appeared sad as he gazed toward the heavens.

24

~

While Eli was in the sweat lodge with Lost Arrow, Sukee, with the help of Willow and Fawn, were preparing Cornflower for her wedding. Cornflower remained quiet as she was bathed and her body rubbed with scented oils. Strips of colorful ribbon were woven into her two long, black braids.

After Cornflower's parents were killed by white men, Sukee had raised her granddaughter. Her daughter, Morning Dove, had been the same size as Cornflower. Sukee had made Morning Dove's dress from the skin of a rare white doe. She had kept the dress in anticipation of this day. Many hours had been spent making it for her only child. It was decorated with hundreds of colorful beads, representing the four corners of the earth: White for east, blue for south, yellow for west and black for north.

Cornflower's jewelry consisted of a neckless made from wampum shells. White and black wampum, had long been used by the Indians of the region. Black was the most valuable, and Sukee had fashioned the necklace of all black shells. It was one of a kind, as was the headband crowning the bride.

Tears filled Sukee's eyes as she admired her beautiful granddaughter, who was the image of Morning Dove, twenty years earlier.

Taking Cornflower in her arms, Sukee said, "You look lovely, my dear. Walking Eagle and I are very proud of you. Your mother's silver earrings are a gift from her. They look perfect, reaching your shoulders as they do."

Cornflower released Sukee. "I will miss you," she told Sukee. "you have taught me many things. Though I look forward to being Eli's wife, I fear how his former life will affect our life together."

"Do not worry my dear," Sukee assured her. "He is a fine and honorable man. I believe he will respect you and treat you well. The spirits are kind. They will protect you." Sukee and Walking Eagle had always been protective of their only grandchild. They were getting older and wished to see Cornflower happily married.

Normally, an Indian wedding would take many days to prepare. The wedding itself would last all day. Cornflower's wedding, however, must be accomplished as quickly as possible, because the army was getting nearer. Only the most important rituals would be observed.

When the sun shone brightly overhead, Lost Arrow came to escort Eli. On the way he informed Eli that the tribal leaders had given him an Indian name.

"From now on, you will be called White Fox. You have proven to be a strong, courageous and honorable man. We welcome you."

"I will do my best to live up to your expectations and always care for Cornflower."

"Handsome Lake, the man you heard preach in Appletown some time ago, is here to perform the ceremony."

"I remember him. I hope just he does not talk as long today. I had trouble staying awake before."

Lost Arrow laughed, remembering.

When the two arrived at the designated location, a sacred circle had been formed. Handsome Lake, wearing a long black robe, stood waiting. His face, seamed by years in the sun, made his eyes appear to to have sunken into the lines that looked as if they were burned into his dark skin.

Cornflower, accompanied by Sukee, entered the circle and stood next to Walking Eagle, Lost Arrow and Eli. First, the bride and groom were instructed to proceed with the symbolic (washing of hands). This was done to rid them of evil, and loves of the past. Next was a meal of corn mush, made of both yellow and white corn. The white represented male and the yellow female, joined together. No words were spoken as they ate.

Cornflower, a few inches taller than her groom, stood patiently by Eli's side. Everything remained quiet until an Indian flute played a love song softly meant to enhance the attraction of the bride and groom to each other. The flute was soon joined by traditional Indian drums making low, earthy sounds as the celebration continued. The tempo and volume of the drums increased, then suddenly stopped. Handsome Lake stepped forward and proceeded to bless the union and all those present.

Blue blankets were placed around the shoulders of both Cornflower and Eli. These represented qualities of weakness, sorrow, failure and spiritual depression.

Each was presented with a wedding basket. The bride's basket contained bread and corn, a promise to nurture and support. The groom's basket held meats and skins, a promise to feed and protect his bride.

All was silent before Handsome Lake spoke. The relatives gathered around the couple in the center of the circle. They proceeded to remove the separate blue blankets and enveloped Cornflower and Eli in one large white blanket, representing their new life of happiness, fulfillment and peace as the Holy Man blessed their marriage.

"Now you will feel no rain,
For each of you will be shelter to the other.
Now you will feel no cold,
For each of you will be warmth to the other.
Now there will be no loneliness,
For each of you will be a companion to the other.
Now you are two bodies,
But there is only one life before you.
Go to your dwelling place
To enter into the days of your togetherness
And may your days be good and long upon the earth."

Following the wedding, the spiritual elders and the tribal officials celebrated with a pipe ceremony. The female elders served corn soup, berry pudding and frybread, as a special treat. Eli was relieved the ceremony was over. It was more complicated and longer than the simple wedding he and Ruth had shared. It had been an exhausting day. He was anxious to be alone with Cornflower.

Eli followed Cornflower, as she walked quietly off into the woods, leaving the celebrating guests. He was tired and overwrought with thoughts of the future. He suddenly felt old. He wished he knew where Cornflower was taking him. Where was the army? Would they recognize him? Would Cornflower be safe with him? So many questions.

Cornflower was happy to be taking her husband to a small log cabin, once built by settlers. It had stood empty until the Indians claimed it.

The building was located in a picturesque valley, within an hour's walk from Appletown. The sound of water flowing over rocks, and the scent of pine in the air eased the tension

Eli had been feeling. A large rock jutted out over the water nearby. He thought it was an ideal destination and began to relax.

Earlier in the day Sukee and Walking Eagle had taken plenty of food, as well as Eli and Cornflower's personal possessions, to the cabin.

"I like your name, Eli. I will not call you White Fox. You are my brave husband. We will be safe and happy here," Cornflower informed him.

They took the white blanket from the wedding into the cozy dwelling.

"It has been a long day," Cornflower said. "I'm going outside while there is still daylight."

Glad for a chance to relax, Eli quickly joined her.

"It's so quiet and peaceful here. Why have I never seen this place before?"

Pleased that she was able to surprise Eli, Cornflower simply smiled, offering no explanation. Eli began to wonder how many other surprises his wife had in store for him. Many things had changed since scouts had reported the approach of the soldiers.

"What is the tradition of your people? How long are we to be staying in this lovely paradise?

"I am not sure, having never experienced being married before. Sukee was always busy. She taught me many lessons about life." Cornflower told Eli. "Then, everything happened so fast, there was not time."

The two sat together quietly on the flat rock, listening to the water flowing softly before them, and birds singing their evening songs. Cornflower sat close to Eli, her arm around his shoulder.

Eli liked Cornflower very much and knew he should be happy the Indians accepted him as one of their own. However, his heart was heavy. He had been a devoted husband to Ruth, and a loving father to his children. He did still miss them, and something in him longed to go home. If given the opportunity to escape when the soldiers came, would he take that chance?

The old one room log house was small. The simple bed took up most of the space along one wall. It was covered with soft pelts. They placed their blanket on top. Some cooking utensils and other supplies hung on the opposite wall, next to a cobblestone fireplace where an iron rod held a large kettle. Additional firewood was stacked off to one side. While Eli was building a fire he noticed a loose wall-board, near some wall hooks holding warm coats. He said nothing to Cornflower as she placed the kettle of water back over the fire to heat.

At dusk, they went outside to watch the beautiful sunset on their wedding day. Inside, the small room was lit by the fire's glow. Everything seemed so peaceful. The air was fresh. Why couldn't life be like this always? Eli said to himself. Time passed. The sun set. When the moon began to peek through the trees, they went inside, where Cornflower immediately began to prepare food. She knew Eli must be as hungry as she was.

Eli sat on the bed and tried to relax while he observed how quickly and efficiently Cornflower worked. She placed a generous piece of venison into the now boiling water and started to prepare vegetables. Sukee and Walking Eagle had supplied enough food to last the newlyweds for days.

As Eli continued to watch Cornflower, he prayed as he had often done in the past. He asked God to protect him, and to keep Cornflower safe when the army arrived.

Cornflower hummed as she worked. Eli was thinking she looked like a beautiful child, as she stood in the glow of the firelight. She turned and walked over to him.

"Are you hungry? Are you happy?" she asked.

Eli quickly brought his mind back to the present. "Why do you ask,?" he answered, as he stood reaching out for her. "In answer to you questions, "No and yes," he said "I'm too excited to be hungry and yes, I am very happy."

Cornflower smiled, took two large apples form a basket and walked outside. The stars were bright as she lowered herself on the rock ledge. When Eli joined her she handed him the biggest apple. Seated side by side, they enjoyed the crisp fruit while their meal was cooking. No words were needed.

As the moon rose higher, Cornflower turned to Eli. "What are you thinking?" she asked.

"I was thinking how lovely you look with the moon shining on your hair. I feel fortunate to have such a young, beautiful wife, and hope I can make you happy."

Eli knew he must concentrate on the present and try not to think of Ruth or he could not prevail. Cornflower was his wife, no longer the shy young girl he'd met over a year ago. Later, he would write in his journal. There had been no time in the past few days to do so. Writing might be a way to help sort things out.

"Cornflower, I feel I have become a true Indian and that I belong here with you." Eli said, as he finished the last bite of his apple and reached for Cornflower's hand. When he put his arm around her and pulled her close, he felt her shiver.

"Would you like to go inside by the fire?"

Cornflower closed her eyes for a instant and then returned his gaze. She seemed to anticipate what was happening, and as Eli held her, she slid her arms around his neck as they embraced. Cornflower felt excited when Eli held her close as they entered the hut.

The Indians gave no thought to being naked. Knowing this, Eli had always avoided undressing in the presence of others. He also remembered that, during his illness and high fever, Cornflower and Sukee had bathed and cared for him. He proceeded to undress underneath the blanket while Cornflower, having no inhibitions, disrobed in unseemly haste.

She slowly undid her long braids and let her hair cascade down her back, over her brown shoulders, before getting under the blanket with her husband. Between the heat in the room, and his increased desire, Eli quickly pulled Cornflower close. When Eli kissed her, Cornflower's moist lips willingly met his. Their mutual desire was all that mattered.

After the long time without Ruth's love, Eli could control himself no longer. Cornflower's warm body brought him to heights he had never before experienced. A night of passion passed quickly, leaving the newlyweds asleep, locked in each others arms.

25

~

Suddenly, the sound of gunfire and loud shouts awakened Eli. He got up and peeked through a crack in the wall. There were three men on horseback crossing the creek. They appeared to be drunk, and were arguing as they dismounted. It was impossible to determine who they were in the dim light.

If not for the moon, Eli wouldn't have been able to see the men as they approached. Pulling on his britches, he watched trough a slit in the wall and saw one man carelessly toss a whiskey bottle which shattered on the rock where he and Cornflower had spent the previous evening. Their behavior frightened Eli. Were they deserters, renegade Indians, or possibly Tories? He had no way of knowing and no time to find out. His first thought was for Cornflower's safety.

"Cornflower, wake up. Hurry. Get dressed. There are strangers outside. They are drunk and look like trouble. I noticed a loose wall board in back of our bed last night. I'll open it so you can fit through" While Cornflower quickly dressed, Eli instructed her.

"Run back to Sukee's house as fast as you can. Don't look back. Stay there til I come for you."

Cornflower didn't hesitate, but did as she was told. Eli held the board out of her way to hasten her escape. As Eli put the board back in place, he softly called after her, "I love you," and wondered if she heard. She was a fast runner, familiar with the forest, and was soon out of sight.

The men made no attempt to be quiet as they staggered around the house. A big bully of a man shouted orders to the others. "Nobody here. Might's well sleep awhile before we burn the place.."

Eli figured him to be the leader, since the other two men appeared to follow him. "Dang, that is one hell of an idea," a second man said in a slurred voice. "I don't feel so good."

As the third man approached the hut, Eli, now fully dressed, opened the door and stepped outside. He noticed that the men wore parts of Indian clothing and dirty torn pants. Eli recognized their army boots, the only remaining items of their military uniforms. The men bragged about how they had burned a village to celebrate.

Thinking the men might be Tories, Eli asked, "Who are you? What are you want?"

"I'm Sergeant Murphy. I'm in charge and I'll ask the questions," the arrogant leader replied as he struck Eli knocking him to the ground. "These two stupid fools call themselves soldiers," he said.

The men laughed boisterously as they grabbed Eli and roughly yanked him to his feet. Eli watched as they entered the hut and destroyed everything, except for a few of Eli's possessions, which they took.

"You don't look like no Injun I ever seen," the sergeant grumbled. "We've met plenty of deserters like you. You're our prisoner now," he informed Eli, as he proceeded to spit tobacco juice on Eli's new shirt, barely missing his face.

Still thinking the men might be Tories, Eli stepped back cautiously.

"I live here with my old grandmother. I have taken nothing from the Indians. My wife is an Indian. They are my family."

"Don't lie to me. You know you stole these things," one private said accusingly. When the second private noticed the broach Sukee had given Eli, he ripped it away.

The soldiers had consumed a large amount of alcohol the previous day, while hanging around a deserted Indian village. While drinking, they had decided to exchange their army uniforms for some odd pieces of Indian clothing left behind when the owners made a hasty retreat.

Showing no sympathy, the men continued to abuse Eli.

"Get moving, you lazy, thieving bastard. We know how to handle the likes of you. Now start running and do not stop until I tell you," the sergeant commanded in a slurred voice.

"But I," Eli tried desperately to defend himself, as he stumbled forward. The sergeant was impatient as they mounted their horses.

"Shut your mouth and get a move on, you stupid fool, unless you want to burn along with this filthy shack."

Eli struggled to keep up. When he slowed, the riders brought their horses close and threatened to stomp on him. He was about to collapse when his tormentors stopped in a secluded place, shaded by large trees. The men were so drunk they quickly fell asleep, seeming to completely forget Eli's existence.

Though he was both tired and sore, Eli's mind was working. The loud snoring convinced him his captors would sleep for awhile, maybe long enough for him to get away. Cautiously working his way toward the horses, he gently patted the one nearest as he whispered to it. The horse remained quiet as Eli slowly mounted. He managed to give the others a slap on the rump as he rode past. All three took off at a gallop.

"The horses seem as happy to get away as I am," he thought.

Eli headed in the direction of Appletown. The two horses followed. As they approached Appletown, he saw no one. It was too quiet.

"Is anyone here?" he called out.

When there was no answer, he dismounted and went to Sukee's house. Normally there would be lots of activity at this time of day. He heard nothing.

"Is anybody here?" he called. "I am not the enemy."

Eli thought he saw movement near his sleeping space, and cautiously approached. There was a pile of blankets on the bed. Thinking maybe an animal made a nest, he carefully pulled the blankets away and was surprised to find Little Bear huddled underneath. When Little Bear saw Eli, he jumped up, almost knocking Eli over with an enthusiastic embrace.

"I knew you'd come. I knew it."

"Why are you here alone?" Eli asked. "Where is everyone?"

"Cornflower got home just as we were leaving. The scouts had reported the army was getting close and Sukee said it wasn't safe. Cornflower cried and pleaded to stay and wait for you, but Sukee said no and made her go with them. Before she left, Cornflower made me promise to hide and wait. She was afraid you might be hurt when the army comes. Walking Eagle and Sukee will take care of her. That is all I know."

Eli wanted nothing more than to rest.

"It will soon be dark and with rain clouds in the western sky, it is best we spend the night here, out of the storm." Besides, he was in desperate need of sleep and he was hungry.

"Little Bear, please take care of the horses while I find something to eat."

Happy to have his friend back with him, Little Bear hurried to do as he was asked. When it started to rain and the boy had not returned, Eli had just started to search, when Little Bear came on the run. He proudly carried a basket of fresh vegetables. He grinned, and his black eyes sparkled while rain drops dripped from his wet hair.

Paying no attention to the rain, Little Bear said, "Sukee taught me to cook vegetables. You rest while I fix something to eat. I'm glad you're back. I missed you."

When the food was ready, Little Bear had a difficult time waking Eli. Seeing his friend sleeping so soundly, he hated to disturb him, but the food was getting cold, and as the wind picked up it continued to rain.

Eli was only half awake as he ate. If anything, he felt more tired and relaxed.

"Thank you. That hot soup was delicious. It was exactly what I needed." Eli said. "Sukee taught you well."

Eli put his arm around Little Bear's shoulder. "The rain will probably stop by morning," Eli commented, as Little Bear crawled into Eli's bed and huddled close to him.

The next day started bright and sunny, but Eli didn't notice. He knew he would miss Little Bear and wished he could spend more time with him. After eating the leftover soup and some dried venison, Eli rolled the blankets from the bed and secured them to the horses.

"You must join Sukee and the family," Eli told Little Bear. "I'm going to search for the troops and return these two horses. If I am caught with them I will be accused of stealing from the government. That is a risk I can't afford take."

Eli hoped his reasoning would satisfy Little Bear. He did not want to involve the boy in his troubles. Locating the army might be the only chance he would have to return to his family.

"It is very important for you to tell Cornflower that I am well. I'm giving you the honor of looking out for her. Please tell her that someday I will return.

"But I want to be with YOU. You are my best friend. Why don't you want me?"

"I love you Little Bear, and have since the day you arrived. This is a difficult time for both of us, with the army getting closer every day. Please, try to understand. Cornflower will need you and you must be there for her. Trust me. It is better this way."

Little Bear's expression changed. Tears formed in his dark eyes. However, because his love and respect for Eli was strong, Little Bear agreed to once more do as he was told. Though it puzzled him, he would do as Eli requested.

"Will I ever see you again?" he asked.

"I hope the war with the Indians will end soon and I can come back." Eli knew he would do his best to keep that promise.

Struggling to be brave, Little Bear hid his feelings, as the two went in opposite directions. Little Bear headed in the direction Sukee and Walking Eagle had taken. Eli gave Little Bear a salute as he turned his horse east and rode off. It saddened him to see his young friend go, but there was no choice. And he hated to leave Appletown behind.

26

~

Eli followed the river, hoping to locate the army. About noon he stopped at an abandoned apple orchard. The apple he picked and ate tasted so good he decided to fill his sack.

Following the sun, Eli traveled in an easterly direction, continuing his search for Sullivan's army. The weather was now cool and overcast. Moisture dripped from the trees as he passed underneath. At dusk, there was a cloud burst. Desperate to keep dry, he stumbled upon what he thought to be an old mining shack, but not before his clothing was soaked.

However, the one room with it's dirt floor and deteriorating roof offered little protection from the elements. Along one wall stood a stone fireplace, the driest area of the room. Insects crawled between cracks in the stone walls, and small bones indicated either humans or animals had been there. A broken bench and a badly stained table were all the furnishings remaining. It would have to serve his present needs, and for that he was grateful. Hunger was an urgent concern, and when the rain stopped for a short time he ventured out to look for food. Wild onions, dandelion greens and a hand full of berries were all he found. A cup of Ruth's hot tea would have been welcome about now. No, he must not dwell on such things.

Eli lay down next to the partially protected wall, unrolled an old carpet left by some previous occupant, that smelled strongly of mildew, and covered himself as best he could. His stomach growled and he shivered. He brought his knees up to his chest and hugged himself tightly in an effort to stop the chill that was consuming him.

Struggling to clear his mind, Eli thought of Cornflower. He hoped she was safe with Sukee. Then he concentrated his thoughts and prayers on Ruth and his family. Where were they? Had she been able to care for herself and their children? How he longed to be back with them, and have things as they were before he was captured.

Never in all the months as a captive had Eli known such loneliness and deprivation. His long hair was dirty and wet, and what remained of his clothing was disheveled and soiled. He was tired and alone, but believed his strong faith would sustain him. God had cared for him so far. For that he was thankful. Finally, he fell into an exhausted sleep.

Following a long, restless night, Eli waited for the sunshine. It came up bright and warm. The heat felt good on his back. He couldn't quite remember where he saw his horse last and started walking. Careful to avoid strangers, he took shelter under trees and behind bushes when resting. He was uncertain how much time had passed, when a figure suddenly appeared out of nowhere.

Eli thought it was his imagination. The elderly man wore a black suit and carried a walking stick and a satchel. His hat, also black, sat squarely on his head, a stark contrast to the long white hair and neatly trimmed beard. He walked tall and proud, reminding Eli of an old judge who was a friend of his father's years ago.

"Hello there," he cheerly greeted Eli. "Are you from around here?"

"No, I'm looking for Sullivan's Army. I heard he might be headed this way." "I'm Pastor Woodward. I travel where my services are needed."

Eli looked more closely. "Wait, I remember you sir. I'm Eli Jackson. I met you last year after being captured by the Indians. You gave me your Bible. I recently managed to escape and I'm trying to locate the army and get back to my family."

The old fellow paused to think.

"Yesterday I passed near what appeared to be a military encampment," He told Eli. "Perhaps they are the ones you seek. Are you a soldier?" the preacher asked.

"Yes. I served with Washington's Army at Valley Forge and Brandywine, until I returned home, along with other soldiers, to build a fort to protect of our families from Indian raids." Sadness reflected in his face.

"I have time to listen, if you care to talk," said the man in black.

Eli thought about the offer. It was good to discuss his situation with someone not involved in his dilemma.

"Well, you see, when my neighbor, Jake, and I were captured, we were treated badly. I tried to cooperate, but Jake fought back and was beaten and taken away. I never saw him again. I was given to an old Indian grandmother, to replace her grandson who had been killed by white men. She and her family have been very kind to me and treated me as one of them. Recently, because the army was reported getting closer, she encouraged me to marry her granddaughter."

"You are one of the fortunate ones. Many captives are abused or killed."

"I believe in prayer. Every day I prayed for strength to cooperate in order to survive. I know I must return to my wife, Ruth, and my children, yet I do care for Cornflower, my new wife."

"What will you do if you reach the army? Will you go back to your Indian wife?"

"I did not choose to marry an Indian. Her family said it would be best when the soldiers came if I would become an Indian," Eli said, feeling dizzy.

"Are you alright?" the preacher asked. "You don't look well."

"Maybe it's because I have not eaten much the past few days." Eli said. He didn't want to admit, even to himself, what a great toll his travels had taken, or what was driving him.

"I'm going in the opposite direction," that Pastor said. "But, if you go over that knoll behind me, you will see a dirt road that leads to a village. Friendly people live there. I'm sure they will provide a hot meal and make you welcome. After you have a bath, a haircut, shave and get some dry clothes, you will feel better."

"I appreciate your help, but I have no money."

"They wouldn't take money if you offered it. Those folks are Quakers and have always helped anyone in need. Take care of yourself now, and may God go with you."

Before they parted, he shook hands with Eli. "I wish you well."

Eli tried to smile. "Thank you, and God bless you," he said as they parted.

~

27

~

Eli headed in the direction Paster Woodward had indicated. In the distance he saw three men walking toward him. Since he was not far from town, he wasn't too surprised. But as they got closer, he noticed they wore Army uniforms.

"That's him," one shouted angrily when he recognized Eli. The other two stood quietly by, wondering what caused the Sergeant to react so violently.

"You bastard," he yelled at Eli. "You stole our horses and left us out there in the woods. Now it's time to pay for your treachery."

With his eyes on Eli the sergeant shouted orders. "You two, hold him while I teach him a lesson he will never forget."

Sergeant Murphy was a bear of a man with unruly red hair and a temper to match. He proceeded to brutally beat Eli, where bruises wouldn't show, not stopping until Eli lost unconsciousness, at which point the younger men dropped him.

"The Tory's our prisoner now," Murphy bragged,

Murphy was surprised when Eli came to rather quickly.

"You stay here and kill white men. I know your kind," Murphy said.

Eli told him, "No! I've been a prisoner of the Indians, and have killed no one."

"Liar," Murphy snapped, as he struck Eli again.

Eli bravely faced his accuser. "I've two petitions to make. That you either kill me or give me to the Indians."

"I'll spare your life with the devil to it," he said as he struck Eli again.

"If you are a Christian-bred man, you should be ashamed," Eli said.

"Shut your mouth and move along quick time," Murphy said, shoving his prisoner.

One of the young men reached out to assist Eli. "I don't remember much about that night," he whispered. "We were drunk. I'm sorry if I mistreated you in any way. My name is William, but my friends call me Billy."

"That's alright, son. I forgive you," Eli assured him, before asking, "How far are we from the army?"

"About a mile or so," Billy answered.

Eli was in so much pain he felt like it was a very long mile before they reached the green. Several members of the same company came running to met them.

"Why didn't you kill the Tory?" they yelled, swearing Eli should not live to take another step.

Eli couldn't believe it when Sergeant Murphy cursed at the group. "Don't anyone touch this man, damn it."

"Is that you, Jackson?" someone called out.

Eli exclaimed, "Good God, is there someone here who knows me?"

Quickly, the course of treatment changed from one of abuse to one of welcome and congratulations, as Eli collapsed in the arms of his Yankee friends.

The next thing he knew, Eli awoke on an army cot inside a tent. He heard wind blowing through the trees and the sound of men's voices nearby. Too weak to sit, he sighed deeply. A young soldier had been guarding the tent's entrance. When Eli moaned, he quickly entered.

"Where am I? How did I get here?" Eli inquired in a whisper.

"You're in an army tent. You were hurt and delirious when they brought you here. One of the soldiers thought he'd seen you somewhere before. You were muttering something about a bath and haircut. I have been ordered to notify those in charge as soon as you were awake."

Eli was puzzled. "A man in a black suit was helping me," he told the soldier. "Perhaps you only imagined seeing someone, since you were very ill."

Eli realized he was wearing only a nightshirt under the army blanket that covered him. "How long have I been here?"

"Let's see, today is Thursday. You arrived sometime late Monday. You must lie still and rest while I call the camp doctor and notify General Sullivan."

"All I want to do is sleep," Eli said and closed his eyes.

When the doctor arrived he found Eli asleep and had trouble waking him. "Wake up, sir. I must speak to you. Can you hear me?" the doctor asked.

Eli slowly turned toward the voice.

"I'm tired. Please, let me sleep a little longer." he begged.

"I'm sorry, but I have orders to examine you. Tell me where you hurt."

"I hurt all over. I'm very tired. Just let me sleep. It is so comfortable here, and it's been a long time since I've slept in a bed."

However, the doctor proceeded to examine Eli. "Where did you get all these bruises?" he asked as he lifted the night shirt that covered his patient.

"I met up with three rough men. Two held me, while the biggest fellow beat me." Eli slowly explained.

“There are questions that require answers,” the doctor informed Eli. As he left the tent he passed an orderly, bringing a tray of food.

Using a wooden crate for a table, the orderly placed the tray, containing hot soup, bread and strong coffee within Eli’s reach. He then placed the blanket around Eli’s shoulders and assisted him into a sitting position.

“My name is Tim Harris. I have been assigned to care for you. Since you haven’t eaten for awhile, eat slowly. You must regain your strength.” He tried to encourage Eli before leaving to attend his other duties.

Eli realized Tim was right and put forth the effort to do as requested. He tasted the soup, the smell made him gag, The coffee aroma was better. However, he only drank a small amount before falling asleep again. When Tim returned he brought Eli’s clothes.

“We must hurry. The general must not be kept waiting. He is anxious to question you. You’ll have to eat later.”

28

~

Tim assisted Eli in getting dressed. The clothes were dry and most of the dirt had been brushed off. His moccasins were dry and stiff, after having been wet. Eli had trouble getting his feet into them.

"I guess you'll have to go barefoot for now. I have my orders. I will help you walk."

When Eli entered the large tent, he found General Sullivan sitting behind a table. Though weak and tired, Eli stood. After the General looked him up and down, Eli was allowed to sit.

"What is your name? Why were dressed like an Indian, and why were you out there alone?" he was asked.

The military brusqueness and insensibility seemed cruel and unrelenting, symbolizing the white man's aggression and will to conquer.

Before Eli could answer, the General continued his questions. "Who are you working for? Are you a sympathizer of the British?"

Eli was overwhelmed by so many questions. He was tired, but wanted to tell what he'd been through. He struggled to stay awake.

"Over a year ago, my neighbor and I were captured by Seneca Indians near our home in Wyoming Valley. They took Jake away. The Indians made it clear what would happen to me if I tried to escape. In spite of their threats, I made two unsuccessful attempts. The third time I managed to get away, and have spent days looking for the army."

A sergeant interrupted, giving Sullivan an urgent message that required his immediate attention. The general turned to the officer standing nearby, "See that this man is confined. I will deal with him later."

Eli was led across a field where soldiers were preparing for battle. A tent set up as a dispensary had just one man on duty.

"Don't let this man out of your sight. I'll come back for him later," the sergeant said and hurried away.

"Yes sir," the private replied to the departing sergeant's back.

Eli was pleased to see Tim and smiled.

"Have a seat, sir," Tim said, offering Eli a chair. "What did the General decide to do with you?"

"I have no idea. He seems to doubt my story. He refuses to believe I could be with the Indians over a year and not escape."

"I believe you, Eli. If you will trust me, maybe we can help each other. My father was a captain in the army. He married a Seneca woman and was killed last year, under mysterious circumstances. I doubt I will ever learn the truth. I would like to live with my mother and her people. When I was about five years old my father took me to meet my other grandparents. When we returned, my mother's tribe had moved, and because of the war I didn't see her again."

Tim continued. "General Washington has issued an order for the army to destroy all Indian settlements, burn their corn-fields and cut down their fruit trees, leaving nothing."

"Indian scouts reported destruction caused by the army east of Appletown." Eli told Tim. "It made me angry. I would hate to see anything happen to Sukee and the Indians who were so good to me. Tell me, Tim, is there anything we can do to warn the natives and direct them to safety?"

"First, we must not appear to be friendly. I have many small jobs around headquarters. As I learn more, I will report to you. It's hard to tell what fate awaits you. We must be patient," Tim explained.

"I've had plenty of practice doing just that for over a year. I'll wait to hear from you." Eli felt he had a friend.

By the time General Sullivan returned to his tent, he had become convinced that Eli was a Tory, and sent for him. Eli was escorted back across the field, one man called out, "Eli Jackson?"

"Yes," Eli exclaimed. "Is that you, Adam?"

Adam and two other army buddies of Eli's recognized him and came forward. They told of serving with Eli under Washington's command. They testified to Eli's honor. He was well-respected among the men with whom he had served.

Overhearing the commotion, General Sullivan came to see what the excitement was all about. When he learned Eli had told the truth he changed his mind and decided to use him.

"It's too bad you were captured and held prisoner, but you survived. However, it is your duty to remain in the service of your country. I need someone with your knowledge of the territory to act as our guide, to help locate all Indian villages in the area."

Eli was not only weak from his recent ordeal, but he had already served his country and been sent home. He couldn't believe what the general was asking of him. He was devastated at the thought of Sukee and her tribe bring eliminated. It made him physically ill.

For a few moments Eli said nothing. Then he stood and faced the General.

Eli stated, "I have always been a loyal soldier. Now, I wish be given leave to see my family and get some rest."

"You have no say in the matter, Private Jackson. You are still a soldier. Therefore, I order you to assist in locating and destroying gardens and orchards, and burning all remaining Indian villages." Eli was shocked. He couldn't believe what he was hearing.

The general said, "Dismissed" and quickly returned to the paper work awaiting him.

Eli managed to utter, "Yes, sir," then followed Tim to his tent where he lay down exhausted, surprised, and very sad and angry.

"I'm sorry, Eli," Tim was angry. "You need time to recover after the beating you took. Can't the General see that?"

"How can I possibly lead the army to destroy my Indian family, Tim? I've come to respect the Indians. They treated me with kindness. I care about them."

"I wish I knew the answer," Tim said.

Several of Eli's friends brought him beef, pork, and good wheat bread, more food then he had seen for a long time. The bread smelled good and the meat was well prepared, but Eli ate only a few bites, because he had lost his appetite.

29

~

That night Eli prayed for spiritual and physical strength. He sat on his cot, still wearing his buckskins. Tim reported that there were no uniforms available and Eli must continue to wear what he had on. Sitting there alone, with his braided grey hair and sun browned skin, he looked more like an Indian than a white soldier. And he felt like an Indian. Maybe his place really was with them. How would he ever manage to reenter white society?

Overwhelmed and confused, Eli still couldn't understand why the general would not let him go. Staying on with the army for awhile wouldn't be so bad, if he had not been ordered to help find and destroy the fields and orchards of his Indian family. He remembered working in their gardens and picking fruit from their beautifully-tended fruit trees.

"Lord," Eli prayed, "I cannot do what is being ask of me. How can I betray the Indians who accepted me as one of their own? Please, be with me through the coming days."

The next day there was increased activity among the soldiers. Eli's bruised body still ached. He had spent a fretful night wondering what to do.

Eli awakened to the smell of greasy bacon and coffee, but no appetite. However, having no idea when food would be available, he ate a couple of biscuits, before orders were given to move out. As a chill frost shimmered like diamond dust on the grass, Eli stood ready to begin what would be a difficult day. He carried a deerskin flask of water Tim had provided.

There were many soldiers in the contingent, men of all ages. Some were very young, but most were seasoned soldiers. Eli was not surprised when the men couldn't keep up the pace he set. Having walked many miles with the Indians, and in spite of the physical abuse, he was in better condition than the foot soldiers.

Soon the first light of dawn glimmered, sending a soft glow through the big trees that arched above the road that followed a rushing creek. The General rode his horse with the confidence of one accustomed to being in charge. He kept his eye on Eli, making sure he remained in sight.

Eli thought about something his father used to say. "Life is an adventure of faith, if we are to be victors over it, not victims of it." With this thought in mind, he conceived a plan he hoped would succeed. It would take time, but he felt, with luck it could work.

In Appletown, Sukee stood in the doorway of the longhouse, reminiscing. Cornflower's wedding was everything she had wished for her granddaughter. The special dress she had made was a perfect fit. Cornflower was the picture of her mother, who, had she lived, would have been proud. The innocent young bride's dark eyes sparkled, lighting her face with happiness. Sukee and Cornflower's grandfather were pleased that she had married Eli. They were certain he would love and protect her.

Sukee hadn't noticed Cornflower running toward her until her granddaughter cried out. Startled, she ran to meet

Cornflower, wrapping her in a tight embrace as she asked, "What's wrong, my child? Where is your husband?"

It took Cornflower a few moments to catch her breath before she could speak. As tears wet her pale cheeks, her heart continued to beat wildly.

"I was asleep when Eli wrapped his arms around me tightly. He said, there were bad men outside. He told me to be quiet and get dressed. I could hear their loud yells as they rode their horses across the creek. I was very frightened."

Still breathless, she explained how brave and determined Eli was, and how he helped her get out safely.

"He moved a loose board out of the way so I could squeeze through the back wall without being seen. I begged him to let me stay, but he insisted I get to you as fast as I could, and not look back. What will happen to him?" Cornflower sobbed as she sought comfort in Sukee's arms.

Walking Eagle, Cornflower's grandfather, was just returning. "Here's your grandfather. He is wise and will know what to do," Sukee said in an effort to console Cornflower.

Walking Eagle hurried toward them wondering what Cornflower was doing home. Sukee, her arm still circling Cornflower for support, told him what had happened.

"Did you see the men?" he asked.

"No, Eli wanted me to get away before trouble started. He said the men sounded drunk, and he feared for my safety."

"If they were soldiers, Eli could have agreed to go with them to save his life," Walking Eagle said. "We have no way of knowing."

The tribe's elders held a emergency meeting. Pipes were smoked as they discussed what action to take. Since Walking Eagle was the most experienced tracker, it was decided he would set out immediately in search of Eli.

Three days after Eli had received his orders, the troops were preparing to break camp. Eli detected a slight movement in the bushes at the edge of the clearing. He couldn't believe his eyes when he recognized the feathers of Walking Eagle's headband. The Indian quickly lay flat on the damp ground as soon as he noticed Eli looking in his direction. Taught to be alert to his surroundings while living with the Indians, Eli was sure the soldiers had no idea they had been followed and were being watched. He pretended to have something stuck in his throat and coughed. Tim was a short distance away and wondered what was wrong with Eli, but had to ignore him. When Eli, who had been quiet, started talking in a loud voice, Tim figured there had to be a reason for the change.

"We should reach the Indian's cornfields late today," Eli said, clearing his throat a few more times. "I never worked there, but I believe they aren't far. They've probably finished harvesting by now. Maybe we can save ourselves the trouble of burning them," Eli said.

He took a drink of water and coughed again, as if his throat still bothered him. Tim looked at Eli and raised his eyebrows in question, but could say nothing.

Walking Eagle heard and understood the message Eli was sending. He had been following the soldiers, but had never heard Eli raise his voice. He knew very well that Eli was familiar with the area, and had worked with the women planting the corn. When he realized that Eli was trying to warn him, Walking Eagle, his feet barely touching the ground, silently raced toward home.

Eli's plan had been to stall as long as possible. Now he would take advantage of the opportunity to save Cornflower and her family. He decided on a circuitous route to further delay their arrival in Appletown.

The general rode up beside Eli and demanded to know, "Are you sure we're headed in the right direction?"

"See that hill over yonder? I believe the gardens where the Indian women worked is close by. We should reach there by evening." Eli moved on without waiting for a response.

The cool air, filled with fragrant fir and pine, gave Eli a feeling of melancholy, reminding him of his Indian home. As he continued to lead the army closer to their destination, he offered a fervent prayer that no Indians would have stayed behind. In their agitated state of mind, he was uncertain what the soldiers might do. He hoped Walking Eagle had understood his message and moved his family to safety. Eli marched on through the familiar fields, knowing he had done his best to warn the Indians.

By the time the troops progressed as far as the field at the base of the hill, the sun was low on the horizon. Eli stopped.

"This field would be a good place to camp overnight," Eli advised. "There is a creek with fresh water for the men and horses plenty of space for the troops."

Acting as if the idea were his, the General issued orders. "Make camp here for the night. Plan to advance just before sunrise. There will be nothing left of that town by noon tomorrow."

That night Eli was unable to sleep. He lay quietly, thinking about what was to happen the next day, when suddenly he felt a hand on his arm.

"Be quiet," Tim whispered. He had crept to where Eli rested on a bed of pine needles. "I have a bad feeling about tomorrow. You must be careful. Some of the soldiers are tired of all the slaughter. They don't trust you and may try to kill you." He disappeared as quickly as he had arrived.

Tim's message heightened Eli's anxiety. He knew he must get some sleep, and managed a few short naps throughout what seemed like the longest night of his life. At the first sound of movement, Eli was alert. He had no appetite for food, or what was intended to take place.

The General and about fifty of his men followed Eli. When they reached the cornfields of Appletown they set many fires. Seeing the flames and smoke as the fire burned the food of good people made Eli want to strike back. He was heart-sick, and increased his pace through the town, hurrying past the longhouses, hoping they would be saved. The only sound he heard was the creaking leather of soldier's boots as they entered the village.

30

There was not a soul anywhere. No birds or other life were to be seen or heard. Eli felt a cold chill as the men followed close behind. He remembered Tim's warning. Eli was sweating as he walked faster. His heart thundered in his chest. He held his breath as they passed four well-built longhouses. Just a few more yards and the buildings would be safe.

Suddenly Eli heard a man yell, "Yee haw," and turned to see the last soldier toss a lighted torch into the open door of Sukee's house. The dry timbers burned quickly, sending smoke drifting high into the morning sky.

Eli was angry, depressed and exhausted. He couldn't move. Of all he had experienced since his capture, this was the most devastating event. Head down, Eli walked on as he wondered where his destiny would lead. Why did this beautiful countryside have to be blighted by war? When they reached the crest of the hill, he looked back. Flames glowed in the sky, as the dry timbers of the longhouse continued to burn.

The tired, hungry soldiers appeared to have lost interest, after weeks of burning fields, cutting down fruit trees and destroying Indian houses. Eli prayed that enough damage had been done to satisfy the General.

With great determination he forced himself to take one step after another and retreated with the troops on the same path taken the previous day. Sudden movement got Eli's attention. He looked in time to see Tim tumble over a cliff on the side of the trail. Eli would have sworn he saw one of the soldiers push him and ran to help. A large tree branch had broken Tim's fall, but his arm had hit the rocks, hard.

Eli eased himself down close to his new friend. Tim had a nasty cut on his cheek, but the main injury was to his right arm. The protruding bones were covered with dirt and blood. It was a bad break. "Don't move," Eli said as, he looked to find something to use to support Tim's arm.

Eli took the wide headband he used to keep the long hair off his face. He used it to brush the dirt away. Tim tried not to cry out as Eli pulled the bone back into pace. Eli put several large leaves over the wound and used a piece of loose bark as a splint. He secured Tim's arm with the headband then placed the shoulder strap of his pouch around Tim's neck, letting his arm rest on the pouch itself. It was crude, but it was the best Eli could do under the circumstances.

A young private, having seen what Eli had done, returned and helped get Tim back on the path. Slowly they made their way over the hill to camp. It was late. It was dark. Everyone was tired. Eli and Tim entered Eli's tent together.

The next morning, the regular soldiers were still celebrating what they had achieved. However Tim reported hearing many of the men, who were farmers themselves, saying they were disgusted and ashamed of the wasted crops. Throughout the day he overheard various opinions as to future orders. When Eli was summoned to the General's tent, he was anxious. He found the general seated at his desk. Without preface the General addressed Eli.

"Private Jackson, you have proven yourself by leading the troops through Indian territory. I hereby release you from further duty. You may apply for your army pension when you get home."

Eli said, "I have one request."

Impatient, the general looked at the little man standing before him.

"Well, what is it?"

"I need warm clothes. My moccasins are worn out and I have a long walk ahead in cold weather.

"There is nothing available," was the general's quick response.

Eli was struck by the gruff reply. Not so much because there were no clothes available, but because of the General's uncaring attitude.

When Eli didn't move, Sullivan looked up from the papers on the table in front of him. "Perhaps Private Harris can find some used uniforms," he then said, "Dismissed."

Eli felt dejected. A physical blow would have hurt less, he thought. He turned and walked away. The troops were occupied and no one paid any attention to him.

~

31

~

Since the day was still young, Eli decided to start the long trip back to Pennsylvania. He requested food and was given rations in a canvas bag, along with a tin cup. As far as he knew Tim still had his pouch. The young private had gone to seek medical attention as soon as they returned to camp. Eli hadn't seen him since. The pouch was important to Eli as it contained his journal, small Bible and a few personal items.

In the meantime, Tim had been looking for Eli. "There you are," he said when he spotted Eli. "The army doc fixed my arm. He was impressed with the job you did setting the bones. He told me those leaves had protected the wound. I'm much obliged. He thought it was clever of you to use your bag to support my arm. Again, I thank you."

"What are you to do now, Tim?"

"I've been given a medical discharge. I wouldn't be much use with my arm in a cast. I'm to apply for back-pay when I get home. The problem is, I don't know where home is. My mother is with her Indian family somewhere in Canada, and my father is dead."

While Eli listened to Tim, he had an idea. "Why not take Tim home with me?," he asked himself. "He and I are both half-Indian and half white at this point."

"Tim, I plan to head south, through the mountains to my home in the Wyoming Valley. Come with me. I'm sure my family will make you welcome."

"Your offer sounds too good to be true. I'm still young, and after my arm heals, I could work and repay you."

With documentation of their official discharges in hand, the two friends began the long journey. Eli hoped they would come to a settlement where he and Tim could work for food. If he was lucky maybe he could get some warm clothes. Tim's uniform was torn, but it was warm and he had shoes. Eli had tied rags on his feet for protection.

Because the two had only known each other a short time, they shared stories of their lives as they walked.

"I spent my early years with my mother's tribe where other children treated me as a brother. When I was six, my white father came and took me to an English boarding school. He wanted me to learn to read and write. He came to see me occasionally, before he enlisted in the patriot army. He was killed when I was seventeen. I followed his example and enlisted three years ago."

They continued on quietly for some time, content to have a companion. In the middle of the day they ate some of the limited rations the army had provided.

"While the doctor was working on my arm, I overheard a conversation. It seemed that a small group of young, renegade Indians had been terrorizing isolated homesteads in New York and Pennsylvania."

Eli felt a chill run through him at Tim's words. He was reminded of his experience years earlier when he had helped build a fort. Not wanting to alarm his young friend, Eli said nothing as they followed narrow deer trails through the woods.

By dusk, they found themselves on a hill, where the forest gave way to an open space, revealing many stumps. Trees had been cleared, and several acres cultivated. A small garden covered a sunny area near a log house. A pile of cut trees was all that stood between the two men and the dwelling. Daylight was fading fast making it difficult to see. There didn't appear to be anyone around. Rather than risk trouble, Eli thought it wise to spend the night in the shelter of the wood pile, out of the wind.

Neither he nor Tim got much sleep on the hard cold ground. A light dusting of snow fell during the night. When, at last, the sun slowly cast long shadows through the trees, both men were stiff and cold. Tim's arm was especially painful as he struggled to move. The doctor had given him whiskey at the time he worked on his arm, but nothing to relieve the later, inevitable pain.

The sun warmed Eli's shoulders when he stood and looked down the hill toward the house. A clothesline with frozen laundry hung on a rope line strung between two trees. He remembered how Ruth used to hang the clothes out to dry. She always brought them in before dark and Eli wondered why this had not been done.

"Isn't that a dog by the door?" Tim questioned.

"Yes, it seems to be tied there. Let's go see if we can get something to eat."

"I heard a rooster earlier, so there must be chickens. Guess they're in back of the barn. Maybe they have a few eggs to spare," Eli reasoned. His stomach growled at the very thought of food.

"That sounds good. I'm more than ready to eat anything that swims, crawls or flies," Tim said, as he started down the hill ahead of Eli.

Eli caught up as they reached the cabin. The dog had not barked or moved as the men approached. The hole between the animal's eyes was evidence the poor creature had been shot. "Probably died instantly," Eli told Tim. The animal was facing the dirt road that led away from the property.

Looking in that direction, they noticed a small mound and went to investigate. Under a thin blanket of snow was the body of a young woman. She had on a long flannel nightgown. Her bare feet were blue. An arrow was imbedded deep in her back, pushing the fabric of her gown tight into the wound. She had been scalped. There would have been more blood had it not been for the cold temperature.

Eli felt sick to his stomach.

Tim leaned over and retched. "I'm not hungry anymore," he whispered, afraid someone might hear.

"We can't just leave her here like this," Eli said. "I'm going to look inside." He slowly entered the unlocked door. The single window let in just enough light to see. To the left of the door, inside, was a gun rack for two guns. One was missing. A small table was set and a pot of stew, a thin layer of ice on top, sat on the cold wood stove. The log cabin had one large room. An iron bed, covered with a lovely quilt, stood against one wall. A carved cradle was nearby, it's rumpled blankets tossed carelessly on the rag carpet beside the bed. Two straight chairs, a table and a freestanding cupboard completed the household furnishings.

Eli looked to see Tim standing in the open doorway. His face was white. He looked as if he was going to be sick again.

"As soon as the sun melts the snow a bit, I will dig a grave. See if you can find a pick and shovel in the barn, while I locate a sunny spot to bury the woman and the dog."

Eli felt the activity would be therapeutic for both he and Tim.

When Tim went to do as he was asked, glad to be busy, Eli took the gun from the rack to have it handy in case the

Indians returned. He was checking to be sure it was loaded when Tim returned, looking worse than before.

"What is it?" Eli asked.

Tim stood mute and pointed toward the barn. Eli placed the gun on the table. "You weren't gone long. What happened?" Tim didn't respond.

Eli hurried to the barn. Near the door he noticed the earth had been recently trampled. He could tell that more than one horse had been there. Tim had followed, but stopped by the barn door. Eli entered alone. As a farmer, he recognized a well-kept barn when he saw one. It was obvious the couple had worked hard to care for their property. Now hay was scattered haphazardly on the dirt floor. There were two horse stalls. One was open. The horse was missing. In the second stall a hungry, agitated mare continued to stomp in the close quarters.

It was at that moment Eli saw what had terrified Tim. A baby lay under the horses front feet, it's tiny head crushed. Blood was splattered on a large beam between the two stalls. where someone had willfully bashed the infant's head. Blond hair was stuck to the rough wood. At the sight, Eli let out an unearthly scream, louder than any Tim had ever heard.

Unnerved by what he was seeing, Eli turned to Tim. "How could one human being do such a thing to another, especially an infant?" he asked.

Still shocked at Eli's strong reaction, Tim didn't know what to say or do. He ached all over. His heart ached far worse than the pain in his broken arm. After locating a pick and shovel among the implements available, he headed outside. Seeing him leave, Eli followed, but not before lifting the baby and carrying it with him. He gently placed it beside it's mother's body.

Eli used a pick to loosen the frozen ground. Tim wasn't able to help because of his injury. As the sun warmed the earth, it got a bit easier. Eli marked out a plot, not far from the house. The sun warmed his back as he struggled to complete a sad, difficult task, making room for both bodies. While he worked, tears wet his dusty cheeks, leaving brown trails of sorrow.

"Tim, go get the quilt from the bed and the baby blanket we saw by the cradle. They will have to serve as shrouds. As soon as I finish here, we will wrap them for burial." It bothered Tim more than he cared to admit, but he was a brave young man and had learned to follow orders.

Tim reached his hand to help Eli out of the makeshift grave in which he had spent most of the morning. After the bodies were wrapped, Eli cut the arrow away from the dead woman's back. Even though she was dead, he felt it would be cruel to cause more damage. The arrow's point would remain imbedded for all eternity.

With the colorful patchwork quilt stretched out beside her, the young mother was turned as gently as possible. Tim used his good hand to assist as they placed her in the center. Instead of a look of horror, there was an expression of peace on her lovely face. How was that possible? Eli wondered.

The baby, a small precious bundle in it's soft cover, was laid alongside it's mother. It required great physical and mental strength on Eli's part to shovel the pile of earth back into the hole. Tim had found a hoe and was able to help push some of the dirt and smooth the surface with his good arm. When finished, they gathered rocks to cover the fresh mound as a monument to the brave woman, and protection from disturbance by wild animals.

The two solemn men stood by the grave, heads bowed. Feeling that something should be said, Eli prayed.

"Dear Lord, bless this mother and her baby. We commend them into your arms of mercy and everlasting life. Bless the husband and father, wherever he may be." Eli whispered, "Amen."

Silently, Eli and Tim returned the tools to the barn. While one spread fresh straw on the floor of the stall, and gave the horse fresh water and food, the other scattered chicken feed in the henhouse. After gathering a few available eggs, they secured the barn door and returned to the cabin. Both men understood what survival meant, and what must be done to get on with their lives, in spite of their sadness.

"I'm exhausted," Eli admitted. Before I fall asleep on my feet, let's get a fire started and fry those eggs. See what you can find in the cupboard." Fortunately, there was plenty of kindling and split wood. Remembering the uneaten stew, they agreed the eggs could wait.

The stove warmed the room quickly. The men tried to relax. It had been a full day even before coming upon the tragic scene.

While the food was heating, Eli secured the heavy door from inside, with a board used for that purpose. He made certain the rifle was loaded and that extra ammunition was handy. Only then did Eli and Tim sit at the table to eat. After Eli said grace and a special blessing for the food and the hands that prepared it, they devoured the stew in silence, grateful for the nourishment and the time and place to rest.

After eating by firelight, they bedded down together in the one bed to conserve heat. It had turned cold and the sky looked threatening. That's all either remembered until the crowing rooster announced dawn. The room was cold. The banked fire of the night before was now a pile of ashes.

It wasn't long before they had a blazing fire. A trip to the privy topped their list, after which the animals needed to be fed. The temperature had now dropped well below freezing. Several inches of new snow had fallen during the night and, snow was still coming down. The ground was covered with a blanket of white, giving Eli a since of purity as it covered the mound of the fresh grave.

32

~

Jean-Paul Toussaint, a trapper, left Quebec on his annual trip south to visit his sister, Marie Claire. He had five older brothers, but only one sister, whom he dearly loved. Jean-Paul was a rugged, handsome bachelor who preferred to walk, rather than ride horseback. He had many Huron Indian friends, and felt comfortable in Indian dress. Wearing a beaded jacket with fringe, rawhide britches and custom-made boots, he was a rather dashing figure. His black, wide-brimmed hat covered his shoulder length hair, the right side turned up and an eagle feather tucked into the band. The most treasured piece of his outfit was a neckless made of bear claws, given to him by the Indian who had killed the animal to save Jean-Paul's life.

The weather was cloudy the first few days. On the forth day a cold but gentle rain sifted down through the heavy leaves, moving along the ground in a mist so fine it didn't even wet him through his clothes. But by evening the temperature dropped and the wind began to howl as he made his way in the densely wooded area. In previous years, Jean-Paul would have found a safe place in a cave or under a fallen log to spend the night. Instead, something made him decide to push on after dark, determined to reach his destination.

33

~

Eli and Tim saw no reason to continue their travels in such miserable weather. Feeling blessed to be comfortable during the raging storm, they decided to remain in the cabin until the blizzard passed.

After cleaning the stall left by the missing horse, Eli covered the floor with clean straw. He transferred the mare, and provided enough feed he hoped would last through the storm. He collected three eggs and sprinkled dried corn, and secured the coop. When Eli hurried back to the cabin, he welcomed the warmth, and was pleased to find Tim had kept the fire going.

By the glow of the fire, the men proceeded to investigate the cabin more thoroughly.

"This big trunk might have some clothes I could use," Eli said as he lifted the curved lid of the heavy oak chest. Inside was a large gray wool blanket and an extra quilt folded neatly over the remaining contents.

"We can put these to good use tonight," he pointed out to Tim as he placed both covers on the bed

Tim agreed. "It's sure to get colder, and they will keep us warmer than last night," Tim agreed.

Underneath were articles of clothing which Eli carefully removed, one at a time, placing each garment gently on the bed. There were beautiful linens, as well as long dresses and women's undergarments. Eli had nearly given up finding anything, when at the very bottom, he pulled out a man's suit made of course wool. With it was an overcoat, similar to Tim's army issue coat, as well as three knit hats and a few pairs of gloves.

Eli was pleased as he continued to check each item.

"Tim, I do believe my prayers have been answered. These things may be a little too big, but I think I can make do. Thank the Lord."

Tim had been quietly resting near the fire, watching as Eli discovered a pair of boots.

"You act like a child on Christmas morning," he said when Eli put on a boot and proceeded to dance around on one foot.

"They are too big, but I can stuff something in the toes and wear them to travel."

Tim approached Eli and he held up a red wool shirt, "Maybe, between the two of us, we could alter these clothes to fit you."

Along the wall near the bed was a curtain. The men had paid no attention to it until now. Tim pulled it aside to reveal shelves containing various items. Dried beans, flour, sugar, salt and dried meat. Eli was quick to spot a sewing basket, just what he needed.

"Look here Tim, thread, scissors and--what's this?" It was a parka with a fur lined hood, perhaps put there to be repaired. Two long, jagged gashes extended the length of the right sleeve.

"Looks to me as if someone tangled with a bear."

Eli thought it must have belonged to the wife. He thought it must have belonged to the woman in the grave outside, and started to return it to the trunk.

"What are you doing, Eli?" Tim ask. "That is exactly what you need. The poor soul has no further use for it. Think about it. That can be worn over whatever we manage to alter"

"Ruth used to accuse me of being too sentimental. Just a weakness of mine, I guess," Eli told Tim, as he unfolded the soft leather garment. He was pleased that it fit over his Indian shirt. The sleeves were short, but he had to admit it would keep him warm.

Moving the curtain further past the shelves, they discovered pegs made from smooth tree branches wedged into the cabin's logs. The first peg held a dark green shawl. The second was a larger parka, also with a fur lined hood.

"I wonder what the husband was wearing when he left?" Tim said.

"It's hard to tell. The weather was probably warmer when he went away. Maybe he didn't plan to go far," Eli guessed.

"I believe we can even venture out in the storm wearing these clothes." Tim told Eli, sad for the reason the clothes were available.

"Praise God for providing what we need," Eli said. "We can soon continue our journey home."

Tim reached into the trunk, not sure why he was doing so. In the far corner there was a small piece of fabric. "What is this?" he wondered, bringing it out in the light.

Eli examined the piece when Tim unwrapped it.

"It's a beautiful, finely carved cameo."

A card had fallen to the floor. The words, "To my baby girl, Marie Claire, from Mother," were written in fine script.

Too engrossed in what they were doing, the two men failed to hear the pounding on the door over the howling wind.

"Hello in there. Open the door," voice called. The pounding continued harder until they heard and went to investigate.

"Who is it?" Eli was asking when a man yelled again, "Open the door."

When he unlatched the door, snow blew in along with a snow covered figure. White crystals stuck to the man's eyelashes and beard. His black hat had a thick layer of snow on the wide brim. Even the feather had snowflakes stuck to it.

Assuming this was the man of the house, Eli stood aside and greeted him. "Come in, come in. We're so glad you're back." Eli said welcoming the new arrival.

The man stepped forward and loudly inquired, as he visibly searched the room. "Marie Claire, where are you?" Then, glaring at the two intruders, he asked. "What have you done to her? Where is she? Where is my sister?"

"You're not the man who lives here?" Eli asked, surprised.

"No, I am not, and what are you doing here?"

"Please, sit down. Let us explain," Eli said as Tim closed the door to keep the snow out.

"If you will take off your coat and sit by the fire, Tim will get you a cup of coffee while I explain."

The man appeared to be in shock as he removed his heavy cap. He stood facing the fire, extending his hands toward the heat.

"My name is Jean-Paul. My sister lives here with her husband and infant son. I need to know what's going on here."

Jean-Paul sipped his coffee and stared into the fire as Eli introduced himself and Tim, and described what they found on their arrival two days earlier.

Not until the full story was told did Marie Claire's brother speak. He ran his hands through his thick hair, as tears ran down his cheeks.

"I believe you did what needed to be done. Thank you for giving them a Christian burial. Where is Jock, their dog?"

"We buried him just outside the door where he'd been shot. It was too late and cold to do otherwise."

"I guess that was best. Thank you." Jean-Paul said again as he settled in the chair Tim had provided.

"Would you care for more coffee?" Tim asked.

"No, I must go find my brother-in-law. However, some food would be be welcome before I start out."

A week had passed since Jean-Paul left. Eli had been in the barn looking after the animals and was on his way back when he saw a man and woman approaching.

"Sorry, we don't mean to bother you," the man said. "Jean-Paul Toussaint sent us. I'm Roger Sherman. This is my wife, Betsy." He handed Eli an envelope.

Eli noticed that Betsy was pregnant, so before he opened it, he said, "Please, come in. You must be very tired." He pulled the chairs close to the fire. While Roger remained standing, Eli read the message from Jean-Paul.

"Eli and Tim, I met Roger and Betsy Sherman soon after I left you. Since they are in desperate need of a place to stay, and knowing you are anxious to move on, I have asked them to live in Marie-Claire's house while I continue to search for William.

Wishing you God's speed, I remain,

Your friend,

Jean-Paul Toussaint"

"What's going on?," Tim asked as he entered, his good arm full of firewood . "I thought I saw tracks in the fresh snow."

Roger stepped forward. "Can I give you a hand?" Without waiting for an answer, Roger took some of the logs from Tim's good arm and placed them in the wood box by the fireplace. "If you like, I can gather more wood and split a few logs before dark."

"I've been doing most of the cooking," Tim announced. "I have three chickens cooking, in case the weather clears and we can head for home."

Betsy spoke for the first time. "Roger says I'm a good cook. If you don't mind, I would be happy to make supper."

Tim got so excited at her offer he backed up, nearly tripping over his own feet.

"Get hold of yourself, Tim," Eli said laughing.

Betsy was six months pregnant and in good health. After a trip to the outhouse, she was ready to proceed. First, she took stock of the supplies.

"Would you three men like dumplings with chicken?'

A three-man chorus answered, "YES."

While Tim and Betsy were busy with the food, Eli and Roger discussed plans to fulfill Jean-Paul's request. Tim brought water from the well, while his new helper gathered the ingredients for the dumplings. Betsy was pleased to find dried green beans on Marie-Claire's food shelf. The meal was bittersweet, as the four remembered the owners of the cabin in which they had found shelter, food, safety and friendship.

"I hope Jean-Paul finds William. In the meantime we have agreed to stay here and care for his property and animals," Roger said.

Eli was pleased to hear that, because he was anxious to get back to his family. "Your timing was fortunate, as Tim and I need to be on our way."

"We promised Jean-Paul we would stay as long as we are needed, at least until after our baby is born, or longer if William can use assistance."

"Tim and I can start out early tomorrow, if the weather clears. In the meantime, this would be a good time to show you the barn."

"I appreciate that," Roger replied, getting up from the table.

Tim began to clear the dishes. "You rest, Betsy," he said. "You've already done a great job. That was the best meal I've had in a very long time."

Eli showed Roger around. "When we arrived, we found Marie-Claire and her child had been killed." He pointed to the grave. "We buried them together." Inside the barn, Eli told Roger all that they had found, and how they had straightened things out the best they could. "One horse was missing. I believe William rode it, when he left to chase the Indians."

"How sad," Roger said, as he looked around. "William must be a good man. He had so much to live for, a wife, a son and a well-built barn and house. I hope I can help him in some way when he returns."

Eli and Tim planned to leave at daybreak the following day. Eli told Tim, "We will sleep in the barn tonight. Roger and Betsy can stay in the cabin and use the bed. There is no reason for them to get up early and it will be more comfortable for her."

"I guess we might as well sleep in our clothes," Tim added. "The two parkas will help keep us warm."

"I made a thick bed of fresh straw in the empty stall and covered it with an old canvas, probably left from a wagon. Before we leave I'll cut it in half, wrap our supplies in it, and later use it as a ground cover at night. I'm sure we will be fine for one night. It's much better than some places I've slept, especially right after I was captured."

"I remember the times I had to sleep with the horses and was called a halfbreed," Tim recalled.

Satisfied with their plans, Eli and Tim joined Roger and Betsy. Betsy had been resting on the bed and started to get up.

"Stay there," Tim said. "We will fix a bite to eat and go to bed early. It appears the storm has moved on. We will sleep in the barn and leave before dawn. You folks make yourselves comfortable. You are the answer to our prayers."

"Meeting Jean-Paul along the way, and being sent here was an answer to our prayer. I'm so tired, I feel as if I could sleep for a week."

Betsy spoke up. "Thank you both for treating us with kindness, sharing your food and making us feel welcome. I'm not sure what we would have done had we not met Jean-Paul along the way. I thank God for our many blessings."

"Good night," Eli said, before he and Tim headed for the barn.

"Good bye and God bless you. Have a safe journey home," Roger shook hands with their temporary hosts.

In the barn, Tim looked at the bed Eli had prepared. "Not bad. This reminds me of the times my father and I slept together when we traveled. You have become like a father to me, and I look forward to meeting your family."

"Good," Eli replied. "Now go to sleep." As he curled up in his blanket he felt the pressure of Tim's body in the narrow space.

34

~

Eli was sleeping so soundly he was shocked when Roger touched his arm. "Wake up!" Eli bumped Tim with his elbow while trying to untangle himself from his blanket.

"Is Betsy alright?" he quickly asked.

"Not only is she alright, she's been giving me orders for the past hour. I was told that, if don't get out here and wake you two, your breakfast would be cold. I declare, that woman wears me out sometimes. She is so happy about the baby that she can't seem to relax. I guess that's the way women behave when they're expecting."

"Ruth was the same way with our first child. When the second baby came along she was too busy to behave that way," Eli assured him.

"Did I hear the word breakfast?" Tim asked as he stretched and yawned.

"Betsy loves to cook. She thought it would be nice to feed you before you leave."

Tim was up putting his boots on, with some help from Eli. "I love your wife, Roger. Does she have a sister?" Roger left the barn laughing.

The weather improved. Much of the snow had melted. The scent of pine and fir trees that bordered the trail filled the air and became more fragrant as the temperature rose. It had been nearly a week since Eli and Tim left the cabin.

In Eli's haste to reach his home in Wyoming Valley he insisted on starting out by sunrise and allowing only one stop at noon, continuing at a fast, Indian-style pace until it was too dark to go further. Tim, less than half Eli's age, was feeling the strain.

Tim looked at Eli. He was becoming concerned for his friend.

"I understand how anxious you are to get home," he said. At this rate you'll collapse before you get there. You won't be much good to anyone if that happens. Why not take a rest, Eli? At least slow down a bit."

Finding it difficult to answer while walking, Eli stopped. His face was flushed and he was sweating profusely.

"Maybe you're right. After all, I'm not as young as I used to be. Since I've been away this long, I guess another day or two won't make that much difference." Tim smiled, happy Eli agreed, and placed his good arm around his friend's shoulders.

"I surely don't want to arrive home looking exhausted. That would upset my family, especially Ruth. For two years I've looked forward to our reunion. I want it to be a happy one."

~

35

The next day, they resumed their travels more slowly. When they reached the Susquehanna River and turned south, they noticed a plume of smoke. Around the bend they came upon what had been a small house, a few large beams still burning. Some distance from the smoldering fire was a sharp post. On it was a staked human scalp. Blood had dripped from the ragged wound and stained the post a reddish brown. There was no sight of the body.

"This is the kind of torture the Delaware Indians are capable of." Eli told Tim. Tim fought the urge to be sick, and kept close to Eli as they hurried on.

The afternoon progressed more slowly. Once again, Eli was glad he had learned from his Indian family to be observant. By late afternoon, when the shadows of the tall trees had become long thin lines, he noticed a few lines appeared to be getting shorter and were out of place among the trees. He quickly lowered himself to the ground.

"Tim," he whispered. "Quick, sit down and act as if we're taking a rest." Tim heard the urgency in Eli's voice and lowered himself next to Eli who appeared to calmly open his pack.

"Oh no. Not again," Eli whispered.

Suddenly four Indians stood facing the them. They were filthy. Eli recognized their war paint. The Delaware. Their shirts and leggings were stained with black dirt and what looked like reddish brown paint. The sudden appearance of the Indians sent chills through him.

"God give us courage," Eli silently prayed.

There was total silence. No one moved or spoke. Tim knew what Indians were capable of, if provoked. He didn't want to do anything that might bring harm to Eli.

When a Warrior, with several scars on his face and arms, reached for his pack, Eli made no attempt to stop him. The contents were dumped on the ground, including his bible, journal and the deerskin clothes Sukee had made. The leggings and shirt immediately caught the attention of the warriors.

The Delaware Indians were warring tribes. Eli knew of many horrendous tortures and murders of white settlers that had taken place in Pennsylvania.

Before Eli could rise and confront them, Tim was on his feet. He spoke quietly, trying not to anger their aggressors further. In his best Indian language he told them he was an Indian. He attempted to explain how Eli was a brother.

"He is Seneca, friend of French Catherine. He is very brave Indian." Pointing to Eli's Indian clothes he told them they were made by Sukee. Eli is her grandson." The leader's attitude changed dramatically. He signaled the others to remain still.

"Sukee you say? You know Sukee? She good woman." The leader stepped closer to Eli and looked him in the eye. "You brave. Sukee like you, I like you. You go. We no kill you."

The Indians turned and left as quickly and quietly as they had arrived.

Tim dropped to the ground trembling. He couldn't believe he had succeeded. He felt lightheaded. His heart was pounding. Eli remained seated in disbelief. "You are either a very brave soldier or one crazy Indian."

Seeing the look on Eli's face, Tim explained, "Indians are always impressed by bravery. That was the only thing I could think of to do, and something had to be done before they killed us. I took a chance and it worked. I believe God was here with us, and heard our prayers."

Hours later they came to a large house with a barn. Smoke drifted from the chimney along with the unmistakable aroma of fresh bread.

"Do I smell what I think I do or am I dreaming?" Tim asked. "I do believe something good is about to happen. Let's go introduce ourselves." He was halfway there before Eli followed, wondering what Tim would say or do next.

Before Tim reached the door, an elderly woman stepped out, a long gun aimed directly at him. "Stop right there," she said. "Who are you? What are you doing on my property?"

"We are passing through on our way to the Wyoming Valley. My friend lives there," Tim quickly attempted to explain.

"We don't need no more trouble around here," she told him.

Tim turned and stopped short, surprised to see Eli was not directly behind him.

Tim pointed in the direction from which they had approached. "We passed your neighbor's place, which had been destroyed by fire. The barn was still standing but there was no sign of any livestock."

A much younger woman joined the first, who continued aiming the gun at Tim. Two small children held tightly to her long full skirt.

"What is it, Anne? What do they want?"

"Sally, your house is gone. The Indians must have set the fire after you and the children came here."

Sally's face turned ghostly white. "Did they see Frederick?" she asked.

Anne lowered the rifle. "Frederick is her husband. When the Indians came and threatened his family, he quickly sent Sally and the children to me. They came through the woods out back.."

Eli had stayed back, watching the edge of the forest for any further movement among the trees. Only when he felt all was clear did he join Tim and the women.

"I'm Eli Jackson," he said, stepping forward, introducing himself. "I'm sure Tim here has told you why we happened to be here. I'm sorry if we frightened you, but after what we've seen, I certainly understand your fears."

"Please, tell us what happened."

Between Eli and Tim, they described what they had seen the best they could, so as not upset the ladies further.

"I'm afraid the house is a total loss. The Delaware Indians have been responsible for destroying property and killing in this part of the state for years," Eli told them, "I had hoped that by now they would have stopped tormenting the settlers. Why can't we learn to live in peace together?"

Tim felt bad for the women. "We buried your husband under the big shade tree by the house and placed a marker there," he added, not mentioning the scalping. "That's all we could do under the circumstances."

Up to this point Sally had listened to what was being said. "No, not Frederick," she cried. "What will I do?"

Before taking her children inside, she fought tears as she faced Eli and Tim. "Thank you for taking time to come here and for giving my husband a decent burial. I don't think I want to stay here. It will be too difficult, but, with God's help, I will manage."

"I'm sorry for your loss," Eli said to Anne and Sally. I've been a captive of the Indians for nearly two years and I'm anxious to get home to my family."

"It sure smells good around here," Tim said, and felt Eli's elbow poke him in the ribs.

"Of course, how thoughtless of me," Anne said. "I baked bread earlier. It's sure to be cool enough to eat by now."

Without hesitating, Tim followed her into the warm house. Eli waited a moment before joining the others. He remembered how he had often been hungry and wondered how the recent tragedy would effect Anne and Sally. He realized Tim was fully connected to sustenance, and thought his young friend had never been truly hungry. Tim simply liked to eat.

36

After traveling an old road, parallel to the Susquehanna River, for several days, Eli was becoming anxious as he neared home.

"Tim, I'm feeling uneasy about seeing Ruth. What can I say to her? So much has happened to change my life since living with the Indians. I hated to leave Cornflower, but I must face my wife and see my children."

"If I were you I would tell her the truth. Tell her what you experienced while living with Sukee and her family. Tell her how you had to marry Cornflower to save your life."

"Yes, that would be the right thing to do, but it won't be easy."

"I promise to support you in whatever you decide to do, Eli. You have become a good friend to me, but this is something you must handle in your own way, the best you can."

Eli had troubled thoughts as they continued walking. When they reached the location by the river, where nearly two years ago, Ruth had stood and watched him leave, Eli stopped. The only sound was that of the river quietly flowing and the songs of birds nesting in the trees. Just as when he had set out. He thought of the good years he'd had with

Ruth. Yet somehow, a vision of Cornflower kept clouding the picture. He offered a silent prayer for courage.

Tim remained beside his friend, giving Eli the time he needed to determine the path his future might take. He sat, relaxing against a tree and dozed.

"It's time," Eli told Tim. "First, however, there is someone I'd like you to meet. Levi Stein is an old friend. He immigrated with his German parents years ago. Levi came from a long line of clock and furniture builders. He is a master wood carver and, became friendly with the Indians while building his house. They found his wood-work interesting and wished to learn. He treated them with kindness and patience. In return, the Indians protected him, making it possible for him to remain safe in his home through all the raids."

"He was a smart man," Tim said. "If more white men had worked with them, instead of fighting and pushing them off their land, things might have been different."

"His place is not far from here." Eli continued. "Before showing up at home, I would like to talk to him and learn what has happened during my absence, before I continue home."

Tim followed, as the two headed toward the home of Eli's friend. It was beginning to get dark by the time they arrived. A well-weathered bench near the door to the house had an intricate carved design on the seat and back. Tim had never seen anything like it.

"It looks like Levi is there," Eli told Tim. "He stays pretty much to himself, but he might have news of my family." Levi heard talking and came out to investigate. "Who's there?" he asked.

"Hello Levi, It's me, Eli Jackson. I've come to see you. I want you to meet my new friend."

"Well, well, I didn't think I'de ever hear from you again. Everyone thought you were killed by the Indians."

“Well, I escaped. I’m on my way to the fort. Have the Indian raids quieted down any? Do you know anything about my family? Have you heard anything about them?”

“Eli, you know I seldom leave here. I stay close to home. However,

several months ago, some folks were passing this way and stopped. They told me that Ruth had died, after taking your girl, Elizabeth, to her grandparents. That’s all I know.”

Eli was already exhausted and, after hearing about Ruth, he slowly settled on the bench. He leaned forward, holding his head in his hands.

“Are you alright, Eli? Tim asked. Eli remained silent.

Tim turned to Levi. “My name is Tim. I believe Eli was about to introduce me. We were both discharged from the army and, since I have no one, he has invited me to live with his family.”

“Nice to meet a friend of Eli’s. What happened to your arm?’

“I broke it in a bad fall. I hope to get the cast off soon.”

Levi looked at his friend. “I’m very sorry about your wife, Eli. I believe you could use a hot meal. Would you and Tim like to share what I have? There is plenty of hot soup on the stove, and fresh bread I baked myself.”

Tim sat down next to his friend. “Levi is right, you do need to eat. After that, you will be able to go to the fort and learn first hand all that has taken place.”

Tim was right. Besides, Eli knew Tim was always hungry, so agreed to accept Levi’s kind offer.

“I guess we should eat a little before we move on. Thank you Levi. You were always a generous man.” As Tim went to help Levi, Eli continued to quietly think about what to do next.

After Eli and Tim reached Forty Fort, they learned from other settlers that Ruth had taken little Elizabeth to her parents home in New England, when Eli failed to return. She had became ill on the trip, and died of pneumonia soon after arriving. They told him that, as far as they knew, Elizabeth continued to live with her grandparents.

Eli's son, Joseph, had left the fort and returned to the family's farm. He had been caring for the live-stock and maintaining the homestead in the hope that his father would someday return. Joseph had worked hard. He'd married young, and had an infant son. When Eli and Tim walked into the yard, young Joseph recognized the changed man immediately, and welcomed him.

When Eli saw Joseph's baby, a merry little girl who had Ruth's blue eyes, he was so happy, all thoughts of going anywhere else left him. He stayed on, helping with chores, attempting, with some difficulty, to live as a white man once again.

37

~

Many years passed, and peace had come at last to the Pennsylvania countryside. Bart, Eli's old black and white dog, followed his aging master to the front porch. The dog had been Eli's constant companion for a long time. Both had grown old. After finishing his usual evening meal of hearty vegetable soup and Indian corn bread, it was Eli's habit to relax in his favorite rocker on the front porch.

As he reminisced in the late afternoon, he remembered moving here to the farm from New England with his dear wife, Ruth, soon after they were married. They'd built this house together. Their children were born here. Eli liked to remember the happy years, before the wars, before he joined the patriot army, before the Indian raids...

He relaxed with a deep sigh as he thought of his long life. He had watched his children and now his grandchildren, growing up on this land. The old farm held many deep memories. Eli leaned back and closed his eyes, letting his mind wander. Bart seemed to sense his master's mood. He moved closer and placed his large, furry head on Eli's knee.

The old man patted the loyal dog, and continued to reminisce as he looked out over the large vegetable garden, where he had spent the day harvesting green beans, sweet corn, and a new kind of crop, tomatoes.

Tomorrow, he would help Joseph's family preserve those vegetables and store them in the cellar, as Ruth had always done. He was sure Bart understood what he was thinking, or something similar, in that way that dogs have. "Good old dog," he said, scratching Bart behind his ears.

He remembered coming home after living with the Indians and learning that Ruth had died. His daughter, Elizabeth, had grown up in Connecticut, remaining with her grandparents.

At that time, Joseph was eighteen. He'd stayed to look after the farm he loved. He'd married early and brought his young wife to live there with him. She died four years later during childbirth, leaving a toddler and a new baby. Eli, still in good physical condition, helped Joseph raise the children. Neither man ever remarried.

He thought of Tim, who had met a young widow from New York state. The woman had two children and loved to cook. After many delicious meals at her house, not surprisingly, Tim asked her to marry him. They moved to be near her family, but Tim still came to see his old friend whenever possible.

Smoke from Eli's worn Indian pipe, a long-ago gift from Lost Arrow, drifted slowly in the evening breeze. Lost Arrow had carved the pipe after he and Eli became friends. Eli often thought of those days long past, and of life with his Indian family.

The tap-tapping of a woodpecker on one of the maple trees and the hum of bees buzzing around the climbing rose on the nearby trellis, were the only sounds.

Eli rocked back and forth and looked out over the land he had cultivated, taking pride in the mature fruit trees he and his son had planted all those years ago. Ruth had enjoyed working in the large vegetable garden and had spent long, happy hours there. By now, the farm had sustained his family for three generations.

Except for Sunday, Eli still worked long hours every day. Sunday he attended church, with Joseph and his grandchildren. A devout Christian, his faith had sustained him through difficult times. Though small in stature, he had worked hard and accomplished many things. He resembled a child, sitting in the rocking chair, his feet lifting off the floor as the chair moved back and forth.

Bart suddenly stood, alert, sensing something, and barked once. Eli could see dust rising down the dry dirt road that ran past his property. He had to squint to see. A large carriage, pulled by a matched team of black horses, slowed. As Eli watched, the carriage turned. It slowly entered the narrow drive, shaded by a row of large maple trees on both sides, leading to his house.

Eli slowly walked to the edge of the porch and stood next to Bart.

"Probably some city folks, lost their way and need directions." He said to Bart.

The large, fancy carriage pulled to a stop. A somber, sturdy-looking young man, dressed in a black uniform, proceeded to step down. He secured the horses' reins as he greeted Eli.

"Good day sir, I'm trying to locate a farm belonging to Eli Jackson. Can you help me?"

Curious, Eli wondered who it could be, as he went down the steps.

"I'm Eli Jackson. What do you want?"

"My passengers are very important people. The man is from New York State. He claims to have known you a long time ago, when he was a young boy."

Eli replied. "I'm afraid I don't know anyone from New York."

He watched as the door of the coach opened and a handsome, well built man appeared. He stood tall in his dark suitcoat, vest and gray wool striped trousers. He towered over Eli as he looked down at his old friend.

"Eli, don't you recognize me? It's been many years, but I will never forget you. You were like a father to me. Remember, you were living with Sukee's family and married her granddaughter, Cornflower. Then the soldiers came and took you away?"

Eli's old blue eyes blurred with tears. He couldn't believe, after all these years, that it was really Little Bear standing before him, a grown man. His coal black hair showed streaks of gray, but his dark skin and wide smile remained exactly as Eli remembered.

"I went to school and got a good education. Now, I represent the tribes at the nation's capital in Washington. I speak to men in high office on behalf of our people."

A giggle sounded from inside the carriage.

"Who's with you? Do you have a wife?"

"No," he told Eli. "That's Abigail. Her Indian name is Butterfly. She is very creative, very inquisitive, always in a hurry, always on the go. She has kept her mother and grandmother busy."

"Her mother. Who is her mother?"

Before Little Bear could answer, Abigail jumped out, full of excitement

"Momma, we've found him. We've found my father."

Eli felt a sudden chill, excitement beyond anything he had ever experienced. Cornflower emerged, her hat in her hand. She was still as lovely as he remembered. Her hair had gray streaks running through the long braids that circled her head. Her large hat matched her stylish lavender dress that fit her slender body to perfection. She was beautiful.

Their eyes met and held.

When Eli was able to speak, all he said was, “Cornflower.”

~

THE END

Made in the USA
San Bernardino, CA
01 February 2014